Donna Shelton is an award-winning author and poet.
Born in Chicago, she started writing at eleven. When she's not writing, she works for an animal rescue organization and fosters animals.

Breaking Dawn

DONNA SHELTON

SADDLEBACK™
EDUCATIONAL PUBLISHING

CUTTING EDGE

Breaking Dawn
DONNA SHELTON

The Finer Points of Becoming Machine
EMILY ANDREWS

Marty's Diary
FRANCES CROSS

The Only Brother
CAIAS WARD

The Questions Within
TERESA SCHAEFFER

Seeing Red
PETER LANCETT

© Ransom Publishing Ltd. 2008
This edition is published by arrangement with Ransom Publishing Ltd.

SADDLEBACK™
EDUCATIONAL PUBLISHING
www.sdlback.com

ISBN-13: 978-1-61651-758-8
ISBN-10: 1-61651-758-1

Printed in Guangzhou, China
0811/CA21101350

16 15 14 13 12   1 2 3 4 5 6

This book is dedicated to my children Reese and Kylie—they are my inspiration for everything I do.

To my husband Rich and my parents Roy & Barbara Locke— thanks for putting up with me.

CHAPTER 1

I open my eyes to the sun shining brightly through my bedroom window. For a minute I am confused. Where am I? What day is it? One of those over-tired confusions that seem to come often lately. The warm sun on my face reminds me of summer; a sweet, warm day to walk barefoot in the grass. Then the heater starts up with a rattle, reminding me of the snow still sitting on the ground and the cold that refuses to break for spring.

The way my pillow billows up softly around my head and my oversized quilt rests heavily over my body should have brought me some comfort, like those times when I would get a cold and have to stay in bed, missing school and sleeping the day away. Nothing seems to comfort me any more. I don't seem to feel much of anything any more. I am numb.

The numbers on my clock radio roll over to 6:00 a.m.—the radio blares some new rock song through half-blown speakers. I close my eyes—I'm just not ready.

Footsteps shuffle down the hall, stopping abruptly at my door. A quick rap of knuckles against the wood then Mom pops her head in, and like every school day since preschool she chimes, "Rise and shine, time for school!" And like every time before, I lie in bed and wait for her to repeat this ritual at least three more times before I finally drag myself out of bed.

A familiar song grabs my attention. The strum of an electric guitar followed by an angelic orchestra and the soft voice of Paul Humphrey singing "If You Leave." There's a gentle tingling sensation in my head—a memory, *Pretty In Pink* with Molly Ringwald and Annie Potts, a 1986 classic teen movie. Perry and I must have watched that movie a hundred times. Although we were born in the 90s, we loved the 80s and everything about it.

Perry. Oh God, Perry...

"That's us in a few years," Perry says during the scene of Molly Ringwald and Annie Potts working in the record store, listening to music and gabbing on the phone.

Perry hops into bed with me and puts his arm around my shoulders for a quick squeeze. "Working with my girl, listening to music, doing what we want and getting paid for it. That's how I see us."

Perry thinks that it would be cool to work at a music store. Sometimes I think that is his only ambition. Sure, it's nice to fantasize about working together and having fun, and perhaps that would be a great job to have during the summer; but I have always wanted to go to college and make something of myself. I know

Perry doesn't have the options I have and I definitely know that with his grades he has no chance of winning a scholarship, so if working at a record store is his dream job, I just let that be.

Most parents would have a problem with their daughter having a boy stay the night. Especially when that boy spends the night in the same bed as their daughter. But my parents know that Perry is special. Since first grade, Perry and I bonded almost instantly. Perry isn't like the other boys. He doesn't like boy stuff. Perry comes from a broken home and at my house Perry is accepted for who he is. I think my parents mostly take pity on him because he really has nowhere else to go.

Perry's mom is nice in those rare times when she's sober, but his dad took off when he was barely out of diapers. His mom often brings men home, some are one-night stands, some stay for a week or so. But none are substitute parent material. Perry is always telling me that his mom would be better off without him. Since she never calls to check up on him or have him check in with her, I think maybe she thinks she'd be better off without him too.

When we met, Perry and me, I was this shy, skinny little twig of a rich girl with no friends and Perry was a feminine poor boy who would distance himself from others because he was afraid of what they would think of him. Most of the nice clothes in his wardrobe were given to him by me and my parents on birthdays and at Christmas. Our gifts are the only ones he ever receives. Perry is like my brother.

The song fades out and Mom pops her head in the door again. "Come on, Dawn. You can't lie in bed all day."

Can't I?

I stretch my arm over to hit the button on the clock radio. I hate the song coming on next and the DJ is just too damn chipper. Why can't they play Expose's "End of the World" or Tiffany's "All This Time?" Something to fit my mood.

I pull my covers away from my weary body and force my legs over the side of the bed. The cold wood floor barely tingles my bare feet. But like a robot, set on autopilot, I have a morning routine to suffer. My therapist says that with each passing day it will all get better. It's been two weeks and the only thing that has changed is me running out of tears. I just can't cry any more.

I randomly grab some clothes from my closet, not even caring if they match, and get dressed. Now comes the tricky part—brushing my teeth and my hair without looking into the mirror. I still can't face myself. With a brush, I stroke my hair back to the nape of my neck where I tie it back with a rubber band. Simple enough. I run the water for my toothbrush with a small dab of paste and stare down into the sink, watching the water swirl down the drain as I brush the morning breath out of my mouth.

Afterwards, I go to the kitchen, where Mom has breakfast on the table; a few eggs, pancakes and some toast. My stomach grumbles as I sit down in front of my plate. Normally I would clean my plate in a matter of minutes while gabbing away about my latest escapade with Perry. Normally.

"Eat something, Dawn," Mom says. "You can't afford to lose any more weight. You'll disappear."

I can't remember the last time I ate. My therapist tells me that if I eat, I'll have more energy to recover. I pick up a slice of buttered toast to take a small bite. The texture is foreign in my mouth and when I swallow, it hits the bottom of my empty stomach like a rock. I want to vomit. I take a glass of water and sip on it. I should at least keep my body hydrated. Mom sits down across from me with her own breakfast, and every now and then I catch her glancing across the table at me. I nibble on the toast a little more, more for her sake than my own.

A horn sounds outside the house. The bus is early today. I am in a hurry to get away from the food and Mom's sad eyes. I grab my parka off the chair and my bag from the floor and head for the door, juggling my bag as I slip on my parka. Before Mom can catch up with me, I step out the door into the cold and make my way down the freshly shoveled pavement to the curb.

The bus opens its doors. The driver looks at me indifferently as I clamber up the stairs, freezing in the aisle as the other kids stare and quiet down. Dozens of eyes are on me, watching me, judging me. I want to turn and run back down the stairs. I want off this bus. And as if the driver could read my mind, the door slams shut. I am trapped. The bus jumps to a start. Nearly every seat is taken as I work my way down the narrow aisle, feet clearing the way, bags being moved into open spots next to the passengers to maintain a single occupancy of a seat. I walk past Brian Kane, averting my eyes as he moves his bag aside to make room for me. I walk on past him. Brian is on the bus early this morning. Normally he is one of the last stops made before school, unless he has spent the night with his friend Gary.

Behind me the whispers rise. I hear my name, but I don't react. I hear Perry's name and I keep walking to the back of the bus, as far as I can get from the occupied seats. I just want to sit alone.

I slump down onto the cold, vinyl seat. I can still feel eyes on me. I don't want to be here. Oh God, I just don't want to be here. I'm not ready to go back to school and just continue with my life.

I want to disappear. Stop looking at me. Everyone just stop looking at me!

I stare out of the windows, concentrating on the world passing by one block at a time, watching the short lines on the road become one long continuous yellow line. I don't want to think about Perry—I just want a distraction from the prying eyes.

But Perry is rarely out of my thoughts. Perry was always among the first group of kids to be picked up in the morning and he would always save me a seat. We would talk, laugh and joke; we had our own language for our own little world. No one else mattered but us. Perry made me feel alive, special and pretty. I felt like a somebody when we were together. How did things get so awful?

It's the week we returned back to school after the Thanksgiving break; there is Perry waiting for me on the bus, all excited and all smiles.

"Guess what I heard?" Perry grabs my arm to pull me close and whisper in my ear. "Brian and Gary were talking about you in the locker room yesterday."

I can feel myself blushing. I'd had a crush on Brian Kane since fifth grade, but I never thought he knew I existed.

"Is this good or bad?"

Perry smiles and whispers again, "Brian was talking about asking you to the Christmas dance."

"And you knew this yesterday and didn't tell me?"

I playfully punch him in the arm. Perry laughs and points out the window as the bus is coming to a stop. Brian is on the curb waiting to board the bus. Brian Kane is beautiful. Tall, blond and handsomely built, and a football player. The best player on the team as far as I am concerned; and the best looking. I can count a dozen girls who would kill to date him. Popular and pretty girls. I never thought *I* had a chance. Let's face it; I am a twig with barely any breasts and long stringy hair. Not exactly a great catch. But Perry always tells me I am the most beautiful girl he's ever seen.

I watch Brian as he boards the bus and walks down the narrow aisle, smiling and nodding. He seems to know everyone. Perry deliberately busies himself with his bag as Brian approaches, then the bus jumps to a start and Brian loses his footing and stumbles into me. I'm startled and I look up at him, inches from my face, and stare into his perfect blue eyes savoring the moment. Smiling and blushing, Brian apologizes in his soft, caressing voice. Then he gathers himself and moves on past to sit with Gary three seats behind us.

Perry leans towards me and whispers, "He just fell for you."

I push him away and laugh at our private joke, then I risk a look back at Brian. He catches my glance and smiles. Seems a lifetime ago.

The bus comes to a stop in front of the school. I wait as the other kids collect themselves and scuffle down the narrow aisle. I follow the last of the kids, keeping my distance, and take my time following them off the bus.

As I stand in front of my school, which looks more like a medieval castle than a place of learning, for the first time in years I feel totally alienated. I've only been away for two weeks, but I feel like a new kid transferring in from another school. It's like I don't belong, like I'm an outsider.

I stand at the base of the concrete steps until the first bell rings and all the kids start hurrying through the doors. I can only stand, numb and transfixed, as the pavement is abandoned. I am simply too afraid to go inside.

The principal, Mr. Dubois, opens the door and scans the school grounds for late or stray students. I just watch him, this middle-aged man in his tweed jacket and brown elbow patches; Perry and I call him Sean Connery. When his eyes stop on me, he forces an awkward smile and comes out to greet me. I meet him halfway up the stairs.

"It's so nice to see you, Dawn," he says. "Your mom said you would be returning today." He touches my shoulder to encourage me to continue up the stairs toward the entrance. "How have you been holding up?"

What a question. How do I respond to that? If I tell him the truth, he'll have me in his office along with every counselor in school. They'll try to force me to talk about my feelings. They might even want me to analyze ink blots. Or they might try to talk my parents into medicating me. I already have a therapist, thanks to Mom. I don't want to talk any more about how I'm feeling.

"I'm okay."

We walk into the school together and he walks with me. "If you need anything, I'm here for you."

I force out a smile, more to appease him and to thank him insincerely, so that I can go on my way.

My locker is on the second floor so I have to make my way up the stairs against the current of down-coming kids, and slowly make my way to my locker. As soon as I lay my hand on the lock, I realize that I have forgotten the combination. Typical of me. I am terrible at remembering numbers.

Perry has the good memory. He writes the combination down in notes for me. Sometimes I lose the notes. Perry taught me a trick though. What is it? Brian's football number—15; my golden birthday—seven; and how many frogs died in biology last year—28. I try the numbers in that order and with a click, the lock opens.

I open the locker, vaguely aware of the second bell sounding and a few kids hurrying down the hall late for class. Inside, along with the clutter of paper and books, Perry's brown leather bomber jacket still hangs from the hook. I panic as I almost look into the mirror hanging inside the narrow door. I tear it down, tossing it to the bottom of the locker.

I drop my bag to the floor, slip out of my parka and hang it in the locker next to the bomber jacket. For a moment I stand there looking at the jacket, imagining that Perry is at school. My heart flutters with that thought. That lapse of thought. What's wrong with me? He's gone. Dead. Not coming back.

I search for a select number of books and folders, cram everything else inside the locker and shut the door, snap the lock back into place and give the dial a curt twist. I am late for class but I don't care. I'm in no rush to get there.

I'm thinking of cutting class when Mr. Dubois appears at the end of the hall. With my first class being on the third floor on the opposite side of the building, Mr. Dubois takes it upon himself to escort me to my class. It's like he's read my mind.

It's a painful five-minute walk with him rambling on and on about psychology, and how I need to feel, and how I need to heal. During the entire walk to class I wonder whether I should turn around and run away, or scream at him to shut up for the love of God! But when we reach my class, I just mumble a thank you and open the door. Social studies.

Mr. Valentine stops in the middle of his speech to acknowledge me with a smile, and from behind me Mr. Dubois says, "She was with me."

Mr. Valentine nods and continues on with his talk as I walk around the cluster of desks and students to sit in the back row, next to Carla Driver. I always get stuck sitting next to Carla Driver.

I would never consider Carla a friend, but occasionally we exchange a few words. Carla is a scrawnier, nerdier version of me. Her long, brown curly hair is always dirty and her glasses are way too big for her freckled face. She always seems to have an odor coming from her clothes. Perry and I have this game where we try to guess what it is. It seems like a combination of marijuana and cat urine.

Once I settle into my seat, I open my textbook and pretend to follow along. Carla passes a note onto my desk. Without looking over to her, I open it.

"Glad to have you back," it says.

I write a simple "Thanks," and return the note.

A minute later she passes the note to me again. "Want to have lunch together?"

Do I want to have lunch? With Carla Driver? Even if my appetite returns, I'll lose it sitting with her and smelling her. Maybe she is just trying to be nice. I'm tired of people being nice, treating me like some delicate Fabergé egg. Do I have HANDLE WITH CARE stickers pasted all over me? I write back: "No." Hopefully that will be the end of it.

Mr. Valentine pulls down the white projection screen and turns off the lights. He has a movie to show us. The movies are the best part of class. I can daydream or fall asleep and no one will notice. Soon after the lights go out, I do indeed begin to doze off.

I think about the jacket in my locker and I can almost feel Perry here in this room…

During a movie in social studies, Perry passes a note back to me while Mr. Valentine is busy preparing papers for a quiz on the film.

"Brian wants to talk with you before gym," the note says.

Brian is a nice guy, perfect in every way, I think. My dream boyfriend. Perry's too, come to that. Brian seems to be talking to Perry more often lately, mostly in the boys' locker room. According to Perry, Brian has been asking a lot of questions about me.

"About the dance?" I write back.

"I think so. Would you go with him? Because if you won't, *I* will."

I laugh quietly to myself. That's one of the things we have in common; we both have a secret crush on Brain Kane. Still, I think I have more of a shot with him than Perry does. But I will never tell Perry that. I'll never crush his fantasy. No one knows about Perry's sexual preference. If anyone in school ever finds out, Perry will definitely be forced out of the boys' locker room at the very least. Perry knows this, so he keeps his cool with the other boys and acts as masculine as he can.

"I'm sure you would. At least you get to see him in the shower everyday," I reply.

That is always the highlight of Perry's day; catching glimpses of the boys in the shower without getting caught. If only I could be so lucky.

After class, we walk down to the gym. Brian is waiting off to the side by the gym doors. Perry nudges me forward saying, "Show time," as he continues on into the boys' locker room to change for gym class.

I walk over to Brian, clasping my books tightly to my chest. I try to hide my shaking hands. I am a bit relieved when he appears to be just as nervous as me.

"So, Dawn... I was wondering..." He tries to maintain his cool posture, but I see through it because of his fidgeting, which I find absolutely adorable. He looks down at his shoes. "Are you going to the Christmas dance?" he manages to ask.

I tilt my head to one side and pretend to think about it. "I guess, I haven't really thought about it," I lie. It's actually been on my mind since the school announced it two months ago. I have secretly been searching for the perfect dress for the perfect night that might never even happen.

"If you don't have a date already, would you want to go with me?"

I can sense he is preparing himself for rejection; probably because it's taking so long for me to answer. Even so, I refuse to sound too desperate by replying too quickly. It's all I can do not to shout "Hell yeah!"

Instead, I pretend to think once again and forcing myself to sound calm and offhand, I reply, "Sure, that would be nice."

I see the relief wash over his face. He smiles, "Okay, that's great."

Is this really happening? Is my dream coming true?

I linger on for a moment, waiting for him to say something else. When he doesn't say anything more, I excuse myself. I wander over to the girls' locker room, so excited I am actually trembling. I can't wait to tell Perry.

The lights flicker back on and I flutter out of my daze. Mr. Valentine is yammering on about the movie I was supposed to have been paying attention to as he passes out the assignments. I look over the paper as it is passed back to me without reading a word, and slip it into my book. When the bell rings, I gather my belongings. I am the last one out the door. Brian is standing there.

"I need to talk with you," he says, walking along with me as I try to ignore him. "Why won't you return my phone calls?"

I walk on, still ignoring him. As we are about to pass the janitor's closet, he grabs me by the arm, opens the door and pushes me inside. In the dark, I curse at him as he fumbles for the light switch.

"Talk to me, Dawn."

The room is tiny and cluttered with boxes and cleaning supplies. There's hardly any room to negotiate an escape and Brian is blocking the door. Irritated, I drop my books down onto a box and glare at him.

"What do you want me to say?"

He looks at me and runs his fingers through his hair. "Do you blame me? Is that it?"

I shake my head. I don't want to respond to his question. I don't want to talk about any of it. I'm not ready.

"Then what? Look, I know my friends were assholes... none of this should have happened."

He gestures with his hands as he speaks.

"I'm sorry for what happened; but I still want to be with you Dawn."

"*I* don't even want to be with me." That seems to come out before I can stop it. But it is true.

Brian is making a visible effort to calm down. Then he steps towards me to take my hands in his.

"We both made mistakes, but it wasn't my finger that pulled the trigger and it wasn't yours either. We can't rectify this no matter how much we want to—we can only move on."

I look up into his pleading eyes and think how bizarre this is; that the one person I've dreamed of being with since first grade is now begging me to be with him. And I don't want him.

The butterflies in the stomach, the tingling from his touch, are gone. All gone. I feel nothing for him. Not anger, not resentment, not pity. Nothing.

"I just can't do this any more." My voice is weak.

"Do what? Date me?"

Brian, please! I don't want to elaborate. I don't want to talk about it. All I want to do is get out of this closet and away from you! What can I say that would satisfy you enough to let me go?

Instead I say, "I just need more time. I need to sort this out on my own."

Appearing resigned, he sighs. "I'm here for you."

"I know, Brian. I just need some time alone, that's all."

But in my head I'm thinking, "I just want you to leave me alone."

He bends down to scoop up my books and hand them to me. I force out a reassuring smile as I take them and he steps aside and opens the door. Once I am free and clear of the closet, I walk quickly away without looking back. Further down the hall I duck into the girls' room as the late bell rings, and go into a cubicle, locking the door. I sit down on the cold porcelain, balancing myself near the edge so I won't get wet. I drop my books onto the floor and cross my arms over my aching stomach, rocking slowly back and forth.

Back and forth.

It is quiet.

I am alone.

My mind is prompting me against my will as it tries to retrieve memories I don't want to remember. Memories that keep coming, like worms squirming and wriggling their way into my brain. I am remembering against my will. I am fighting the worms in my head. I know it would be so much easier if I just gave in and let the memories run their course, then it would be done and over with.

I feel like I am in a nightmare and I can't wake up. If only I could wake up, I would have my best friend and my handsome boyfriend. I would be happy. I would be feeling butterflies and chills. I can't remember what they feel like. I want to remember. Would it make a difference if I could remember?

CHAPTER 2

I'm thinking back. The night of the Christmas dance was the best night of my life. Perry and me were upstairs in my room, adding the finishing touches to my hair. Brian was down in the foyer waiting for me.

Perry is a great hairstylist. He would even style Mom's hair every now and then. Perry was wearing Dad's old tux and although it was a little too big, Perry looked like a perfect gentleman. I donned a yellow satin strapless dress I bought through the Macy's catalog and Perry said I looked just like a Disney princess. And for the first time in my life, I felt like a princess...

"I envy you," Perry says as he sprinkles small yellow flowers throughout my hair. "Can I pretend that Brian is my date too?"

I laugh. "We're all going together."

"I know. I just feel like a third wheel."

I turn and look at him. "Without my third wheel, I couldn't drive."

Yeah, it was kind of corny, but it was true. I had come to depend on Perry a little too much, I guess.

I stand up and do a quick "look at me" twirl and then Perry offers his arm for me to take. After all, a princess needs an escort, doesn't she?

We walk downstairs where Brian is waiting. I watch Brian as I descend the stairs, his eyes open wide as he catches his breath. I am excited and nervous at the same time. The butterflies in my stomach are flying wild and I am feeling a bit light-headed; but oh, Brian looks so good in his tux.

All three of us have to take a few minutes to pose for Mom's pictures. I think this is as big a night for her as it is for me. As we bundle up in our coats, Dad is giving us a short safety lecture about drinking and being responsible. Basically, he's telling us not to do all the stuff he and Mom did on their prom night. But I won't go into detail about that, because I still can't face the fact that my parents still have sex. I want to think that adults only have sex to have kids and once the kids arrive, that's the end of it. I still like to think like that, even though I know different. That night when I caught them in "the act," the night before I started high school, traumatized me.

When at last we made our escape, we went out into the cold night air to climb into the white stretch limo. Brian's parents had rented it for the occasion. Inside the limo there was Gary Garrison, Brian's best friend, and his date Terri Morganstein. We all knew each other. Never spoke to each other, but we co-existed peacefully enough.

"What's up Perry?" Gary says, putting his arm around Terri. "Where's your date?"

Perry looks at me sheepishly, "I'm the third wheel tonight."

"You should hook up with Carla Driver. She'll be there."

Perry and I exchange amused smiles. "I don't think so," he says.

"Suit yourself." He looks to Brian. "Hey man, didn't you forget something?" He points to Terri's corsage.

"Oh." Brian leans forward to get into the little refrigerator.

I look over to Perry and catch him staring fixated on Brian's butt. For a minute, I got a bit jealous that my best friend was checking out my date. When Brian sits back with the corsage in his hand, Gary speaks up.

"Hey man," he says to Perry. "Were you checking out Brian's ass?"

Perry snaps his head up and looks at Gary. "No!" He feigns disgust.

Brian looks at Perry. He seems more confused than anything.

"Brian, he was staring at your ass, man." Gary insists.

"No, I wasn't!" Perry shoots back. "I wasn't looking at anything. I was just daydreaming."

"Yeah. About Brian's ass."

"Knock it off Gary," Brian says firmly. "Leave him alone."

"Brian, I wasn't looking—"

"I know you weren't bro. He's just being an asshole."

Gary huffs and turns his attention back to Terri, who is giggling through it all. Brian turns to me and takes the pink and white corsage from the plastic box. I put out my hand for him to slip it onto my wrist.

"I can't believe I almost forgot this," Brian says.

"I love it," I say and reach over to show Perry, who acknowledges the corsage with a little smile then occupies himself by staring out the window.

On the drive to the dance, we talk about stuff and Perry keeps watch out the window, deliberately keeping out of any conversation. I can tell that he has been embarrassed. And I know Perry well enough to know that this won't just pass in a heartbeat. It will eat him up inside for days.

When the driver pulls up to the gym entrance, we all file out of the limo. I take Brian's arm and when I reach for Perry as he steps out, he just looks away.

Actually, that hurt me a little. But then Gary and Terri are standing beside us, and we walk up the steps and into the gym where the dance is already in full swing. For a minute we stand in the entrance and scan the room, noting who is there, and where.

We find a table off to the side to claim as our own. Perry pulls out a chair for me and we sit down alongside Terri as Brian and Gary go off to get us drinks.

When Brian returns, he's only brought drinks for the two of us. I want to say something when I notice that Perry appears lonely and hurt, but Perry gets up to get a drink of his own. I wonder what's going through Perry's mind. Even if Perry is pretending to himself that he is out on a date with Brian, does he really think that Brian thinks of it that way?

I sip my punch as I look around at all the kids I never thought I would voluntarily be in the same room with. Perry comes back a few minutes later with his drink and a slice of white cake. I am chatting with Brian about the choice of music being played by a local band and next thing I know, Perry's floating a fork loaded with white cake in front of my face.

"Some sweets for the sweet?" Perry says.

I take the bite, feeling somewhat annoyed that he had interrupted my conversation. But I'm also annoyed that I'm going to have to try to include Perry in my date somehow. Maybe a third wheel isn't going to work out after all. I just swallow and smile and turn back to Brian.

"Wanna dance?" Brian asks as the band starts a slow number.

Oh the butterflies! I take his hand and follow him out onto the dance floor. Brian puts his arms around my waist and I put mine around his neck. Slowly we rock side to side, staring into each other's eyes. I can feel his heart beating against mine. All I can think is that heaven couldn't be better than this.

I close my eyes and touch my forehead to his. The butterflies have gone, leaving just a kind of tingling sensation in their wake. Brian is so warm and he smells so good. I just want to lock my arms around him and forget about everyone else in the gym. I can't believe I'm dancing with the one person I thought I could never have. I am melting in his arms all through this song and well into the next.

But then halfway through the next song, Perry is tapping on Brian's shoulder, asking if he can cut in. A state of bliss interrupted. I am annoyed. Brian hesitantly obliges, probably because he wants to be nice to Perry because Perry is my friend. I try to smile and watch as Brian walks back to our table as I continue the dance with Perry.

"What are you doing?" I say once Brian is out of earshot. I really don't want to snap at him like that, but I am so annoyed I can't control myself.

"I'm dancing with my girl." He looks bewildered. "Am I doing something wrong?"

I can tell by the look on his face that he knows what he is doing. He is jealous that I am dating *his* crush and that *his* crush was getting all of my attention.

"You have been acting weird since the limo ride." Actually, since before the limo ride, but I don't feel like going into detail. "Every time I get Brian's attention, you interrupt."

We suddenly stop dancing and he takes a step back. "Am I bothering you?"

"What is your problem?"

"My problem? I'm sorry I wanted to have a good time with my best friend." Perry looks around and notices he's drawing attention to himself. "Sorry if I'm ruining your night."

I grab him by the arm when he tries to walk away. "I'm not trying to get rid of you. I just wanted some time alone with Brian."

"Fine, whatever."

"Are you mad because you got caught checking out my date?"

His face turns red. That answers the question.

"You need to be more careful," I say. "These guys will make your life a living hell if they find out."

"I know," he says irritably. "I slipped. I'm just tired of… never mind."

Perry steps back up to me and we finish the dance, but neither of us enjoys it.

Back at the table Carla Driver is sitting next to Brian and they both look up when we return. Carla smiles at Perry and asks him if he will dance with her. Perry looks from Brian to me, confused.

"I've been here for two hours and haven't danced yet," Carla says, stepping around the table to Perry, holding out her arm for him to take. Perry glances from her arm to me.

"That would be fun Perry, go ahead," I say.

Perry looks at me like a whipped puppy and takes her arm, with forced gaiety. I feel a pang of guilt but at the same time relief.

I can have some uninterrupted time with Brian. I know Perry will make me pay for this later, but I am going to make it worth it. At least Carla doesn't smell like cat pee tonight.

I turn to Brian. "Did you arrange that?"

"I thought it would be in everyone's best interest."

Brian seems to be sincere. At least if Perry appears to be dancing with a girl, anything Gary might want to spread about the "staring" incident can be laughed away. I'm beginning to see Brian in an even brighter light.

For the rest of the night Brian is all mine. Every now and then I catch a glimpse of Perry dancing or sitting with Carla at another table. But he doesn't bother us. At the end of the night I find out that Perry left the dance early, to find his own way home. I feel a combination of guilt and relief. I'm not entirely comfortable with that.

When I get home, Brian walks me up to my door. We shyly murmur our goodnights and I receive my first kiss. He hesitantly, yet gently, presses his lips onto mine and for those few seconds, I feel a chill shimmer up my spine. A perfect ending to a perfect night.

As I watch him step into the limo, watch the limo glide off into the night, I just stand for a few seconds to savor the moment. My lips still tingle from his kiss and the chills up my spine are only slowly fading away. The cold finally gets the best of me. I pull out my key to the front door and stop when I hear a noise. I look around in the dark and see someone in the shadows at the corner of the house. The snow on the ground illuminates the night enough for me to see that it's Perry. And walking unsteadily, with a small bottle of whiskey in his hand.

"What are you doing?" I say as he approaches me in his drunken stupor.

"Celebrating your first boyfriend," he slurs and turns the bottle up to drain the last of its contents. He tosses the bottle across the garden where it skips across the snow and shatters on the shoveled pavement.

"You're drunk."

I am completely surprised. That's one thing we never do—drink alcohol. Mostly because his mom is such an alcoholic. Perry has always been turned off by the stuff. The night—which had been heavenly for me— had obviously been hell for him.

"Come in, you can sleep it off."

He falls against me in his drunken stupor, nearly knocking me over with his weight.

"I love you—you know that, right?" Perry slurs.

"I know."

I open the door and help him inside. I'm not about to scold or argue with a drunken Perry. I don't know what to expect from a drunken Perry. I'm not too eager to find out.

"You are so lucky to be you," he says. I stumble with him over to the couch, where he falls over the arm backwards onto the cushions.

Before I am done wrestling his shoes off, he is out cold and snoring loudly. I cover him with a blanket, lock up the house and creep upstairs, past my parents' room, to mine. As I slip out of my princess dress and into some flannel pajamas, I touch the soft petals of the corsage with the tips of my fingers. I'm struggling with my good feelings of this dreamy night and my guilt over Perry.

All the same, I drift into sleep, playing back all the moments with Brian in my mind. I omit Perry's disruptive behavior, of course, and my last memory as I fall asleep is the sensation of Brian's lips on mine.

In the morning I go down to breakfast to find Perry already sitting at the table with my parents. Dad looks me over with an arched brow, like he's trying to work out if I'm sober.

"You kids must have had a good time last night," Dad says, looking over to Perry who is trying to hide his hangover and failing to do it.

Perry smiles sheepishly as I sit down across from him and his cup of coffee and plain toast. Perry isn't a coffee drinker, I know, but Dad has had his share of hangovers in the past and he knows a cup of coffee and plain toast will do Perry good.

My Mom and Dad don't support teenage drinking, but they understand that teenagers make mistakes. They know the home Perry comes from, and they don't want to get angry with him or say anything that might scare him away. They know what our family means to him. My parents are cool in their own way.

Later in the morning, Perry changes back into his own clothes. We've been watching some television in the living room for about an hour when the phone rings. Mom comes in and hands me the phone. It's Brian.

"I wanted to ask if you were doing anything today…"

It's nice to hear his voice. It proves that last night wasn't just a dream. I'm thrilled that he's called me and I can't wait to see him again. But even I know that I shouldn't sound too desperate.

"Just my usual winter Saturday," I tell him, "which basically means veging out on the sofa in front of the television."

"Would you want to see a movie with me this afternoon?" Brian hesitates. There's an air of uncertainty in his voice. "Just the two of us?"

My heart flutters and I want to screech in the kind of girlie excited way that usually annoys me. Of course I want to see a movie with him, and as for his comment about just the two of us? I know exactly what he means. And it's fine by me.

"Sure."

"Great. My dad's letting me borrow his car. I'll pick you up at noon."

"I didn't know you could drive."

"I passed last week. But don't worry, I'm a good driver."

"That's what they all say." I laugh.

As soon as I put the phone down, Perry gives me *the look*. He wants me to feel like I'm abandoning him. I guess that in a way, I am.

"He speaks loud enough on the phone," Perry says.

"You heard?"

Again *the look*. Then he takes the remote and starts flipping through the channels. I refuse to let him ruin this for me. I'm sure that once Perry gets a boyfriend, he will want to spend as much time with *him* as possible too. This is just the beginning of my first relationship, I don't want to do anything to stunt its growth. Does he expect me to stay single and all his forever?

"It's not like I'm going to spend the entire day with him." I want to reason with him and be able to leave without him making me feel guilty. "We can do stuff later and maybe I'll come back with some juicy gossip."

Perry seems to soften his glare with that. "I do want to check out that new store at the mall," he says. "And maybe we can grab a bite to eat."

"It's a date."

Although I am desperate to leave right away, I don't want it to appear that way. So I spend another long hour with Perry, watching some cheesy B-rated sci-fi movie, which is actually our weekend norm. But I don't enjoy it as much as I normally would. I would usually be making fun of the bad acting, but I am too distracted, thinking about my date. What can I wear? What will it be like sitting in a dark theater with

Brian, sharing popcorn and holding hands?

After a while I go upstairs to get dressed and apply some light makeup. A white hooded sweater and some khakis, and my hair pulled up into a loose pony tail. Yeah, I look good.

Perry leaves just minutes before Brian arrives. My parents are uncomfortable about sending me off with an inexperienced driver so I have to stand idly by as Dad speaks to Brian about his driving experience and safety issues. Dad obviously isn't going to let some inexperienced teenager take off with his baby girl without giving him the third degree. I am somewhat amused by it all. However, Brian's a smooth talker and he knows how to work my parents so that they feel at ease. I find myself impressed by his tact.

Well, Saturday doesn't turn out exactly as I imagine. Brian and I end up seeing a movie, going to lunch at the mall, doing a little bit of shopping and afterwards I go back to his house for dinner, where I meet his parents and his little sister. His parents are the ritzy type, but they are very nice to me. His sister is, well, a prissy little eight-year-old who acts out against my presence in her home. It is interesting.

It's almost nine o'clock when Brian takes me home. The day has gone by so fast and I just don't want it to end. We kiss goodnight—for about five minutes—in his car, and I finally go inside to find my parents in the living room. They are livid. Mom is looking at me and shaking her head disapprovingly.

"Perry waited here two hours for you and you couldn't even call?" Mom stands up and crosses her arms over her chest. She looks at me with her bug-eyed, tight-lipped expression. The one I get whenever she is upset with me.

Okay, I screwed up. What could I say that would make this better?

"I'm sorry."

Why does everyone have to make me feel bad for spending time with Brian?

"I lost track of time. I'll call Perry in the morning."

"He's very upset with you," Dad says, keeping his composure better than Mom. "You should never just ditch your friends like that. Especially for a boy you've only just started seeing."

I am waiting for this. Here is the problem; my parents like Perry because my virginity is never threatened when I'm with him. And with Brian, well, that's a totally different story.

"Brian seems like a... nice boy," Mom says. "But maybe we should have a little talk first, before you see him again."

And here is where Mom follows me up to my room for a *girl talk*. Mom went into detail. I think she was trying to scare me away from the very thought of having sex, and I listen and nod and respond the way I think she expects me to. All the while I am wondering how it can be that my happiness is bringing such misery to others? Who has the problem here? All I want is to spend time with my boyfriend and do typical teenager stuff. Why should that upset people?

The next morning I call Perry's house and leave half a dozen messages on his machine. He's mad at me. I wait until the afternoon and when he doesn't return any of my calls, I call Brian and talk on the phone for about an hour with him.

Brian wants me to come hang out with him, but I doubt my parents would like that very much, especially after yesterday. I tell him they are upset with me for coming in late and not calling, but I don't go into any details. Instead, I decide to take a walk over to Perry's house, nearly half a mile away. I bundle up in my parka, gloves and scarf, but it is still too cold for my liking. In warmer weather, it's not such a bad walk, but the bitter wind makes it unbearable today.

When I get to Perry's one-story brick bungalow, I knock on the front door. No answer. I knock again, even harder. I think I see the blinds move, but no one answers. Yeah, he's mad at me.

It's far too cold for me to wait outside. If he can't get over his anger and let me in, I'm not going to beg. It's too cold to mess around.

I walk on for a few more blocks to the public library, where I go inside to warm up. I call Brian on my cell and I ask him to come pick me up if he can. I'm not going to waste my day trying to get Perry to talk to me. Once he's had time to cool off, I'll try again, but for now, I'm going to embrace the day.

CHAPTER 3

Monday morning, I'm standing on the curb waiting for the school bus and feeling like a new person. I am confident, energized and up on my pedestal. I feel like this is the me I always wanted to be. I wonder what Perry will think of this new me. But I feel too good and I don't want Perry to ruin my mood. I am fairly certain he is still angry with me; and Perry can carry a grudge for a long time. I know this from experience. Even best friends get angry with each other from time to time.

When the bus arrives and those narrow doors creak open, the driver gives me the usual indifferent stare. But I feel an inner confidence that I'm sure everyone notices as I walk down the narrow aisle towards Perry. I hover, hesitating by the free seat next to him.

"Is this seat taken?" I ask, as if he were a stranger.

He forces out a weak smile and shakes his head. "This is still your seat."

I sit down next to him. I feel a little uncomfortable, but I want to clear the air. I don't want him to be mad at me and I don't want to feel guilty.

"As friends go... I know I've sucked lately and I'm sorry."

He shrugs, "I'm over it. I don't have the energy to be mad any more."

"My energy's pretty depleted too." I am relieved we can move on. We can at least act as though there was never a problem between us.

We talk on through the stops but when it comes to Brian's house, Perry gets quiet. I try to appear indifferent as Brian boards the bus. He keeps his eyes on me the entire time, smiling as he makes his way down the aisle. He sits a few seats behind us, next to Gary. I have to fight an urge to run back and sit across from him. I want to so bad! But Perry would never forgive me if I abandoned him on the bus too.

Over the following few weeks, and even through the Christmas break, balancing my relationships with Perry and Brian is a struggle. At times I feel pretty high on life, with two handsome boys demanding my attention. What girl wouldn't enjoy that? With Perry, it is always just the two of us, solitary teenagers, messing around and having fun. With Brian, I am slowly working my way into his clique—the popular kids. Perry hates the popular kids.

As I start to socialize with Brian's clique more, I begin to feel an invisible wall come between Perry and me. I can't even talk about any of my new friends without a wisecrack or downright insult from Perry. Eventually, when I get the hint—well, several hints—that he doesn't want to talk about any of my new friends, I don't talk much about anything. I don't know what to talk about. It's almost as if I've completely forgotten the things that Perry and I used to enjoy talking about and doing together. My mind is always on the fun I have with Brian and my new friends. Perry has become more of a guilty obligation than anything.

I can't recall exactly when this change of feeling occurred. The feelings that I thought I would have forever with Perry were suddenly diminishing. Although I still love him and want him in my life, I've become tired of constantly choosing between my friends and him, and watching what or who I talk about around him. My only wish is for everyone to get along, so we can all hang out together and I can stop dividing up all my time and energies. Perry won't hear of it though. He just won't consort with Brian or his friends in any way, manner, shape or form.

I am exhausted.

One day, I am over at Perry's house—a very rare event, but his mom is off with a boyfriend for the weekend and he has the house to himself. It is a nice house on the outside, but the inside could really use some work. I know Perry tries his best to keep his house from looking like a pig sty. His mom definitely doesn't care. Perry has more burdens than a fifteen-year-old should have to bear. But at least with his mom gone for the weekend, he is free to be himself.

I've brought a bag of groceries over for us to share since his mom hasn't left him any money and the fridge is nearly empty. Actually, I guess the fridge would be considered full if I counted all the rotten food that should have been in the garbage. Sometimes I feel like Perry's mom expects me and my parents to take care of him.

Normally I like it when his mom has gone and we have the house to ourselves. Even though it gets incredibly boring with no cable and just a pair of rabbit ears and bad reception. This time is different. I just don't want to stay as long as I used to. I want to go so much that it shows.

After we finish our lunch of grilled cheese sandwiches and tomato soup, I become restless. I don't want to appear restless, but I do suck at hiding it. Just when I am about to tell him I am ready to leave, he takes my hand and pulls me up off the couch, where we are eating and watching fuzzy television.

"I want to show you something," Perry says.

I follow him to his room. He has a small bedroom. Clothes cover the floor, and vintage movie posters plaster the wall—*Pretty In Pink*, *St. Elmo's Fire*, *The Breakfast Club*, and just about everything with Molly Ringwald in it. His bed is a mess of sheets, clothes and magazines. Off in a corner is an old desk with small piles of paper. He has been writing a story about his life—about being a gay teenager and coping with an alcoholic mom. He wants to show me that he's finally finished it. All 387 pages.

"I want you to be the first to read it and give me your opinion."

I smile. I'm happy that he's finished it. He's been working on this for two years. Perry is a good writer and I always enjoy reading the things he writes about. I used to try to encourage him to work for the school newspaper, but he hates just about every student on the newspaper's staff. If he could only get over hating those kids, he would be a great asset for the newspaper. He'd have to get them to like him too.

"Can I take it home with me? You know I can't read all this right now."

"Yeah, go ahead. Just don't let anyone else see it. There's some really personal stuff in there that I don't want anyone else to see."

"It won't leave my bedroom."

Brian comes over later that night. He has a social studies assignment that he says he needs help with. Actually, this is just the excuse he needed to get out of babysitting his little sister. And to spend some time with me in my room. We lay out the books and papers on my desk and as far as my parents are concerned, it's just homework. We actually spend the time making out, with the radio on to cover all the giggling. After a couple of hours I step out to get us drinks from the kitchen. Mom is at the sink washing the dishes.

"How's it going up there?" she asks.

I don't know if GUILTY is printed boldly on my forehead or if she has a sixth sense, but I get the feeling that she knows we're not studying.

"It's good." I avoid eye contact as I dive into the fridge to pull out two cans and check out the shelves for snacks.

"I was a teenager once too, you know," Mom says.

I risk a glance her way. She knows and it's obvious. I wonder if I can pick up where I've left off with Brian, knowing that she knows.

"I know." I just want to make a quick exit without giving her a reason to follow me back upstairs or to come knocking on the door. "You know, as teenagers go, I'm pretty responsible."

She drops the dishcloth in the sink and looks at me, forcing out a half smile. "I know."

Before I can make my escape, the phone rings. It's Perry. He wants to come over because he's lonely in an empty house. He sure has rotten timing. I talk with him for a few minutes and tell him that Brian and I are studying up in my room. He goes quiet.

"For how long?"

"I don't know." I'm tired of cutting my time short with Brian, just for Perry.

He is silent for a long time. I don't know what else to say. I just want to go back up to my room to continue where I left off with Brian.

"Fine. Go have your fun, I'll be okay on my own."

I've had enough of the emotional blackmail and I snap. "You know what Perry? I'm tired of dividing up my time between everyone and I'm tired of you making me feel bad for having a boyfriend."

There, I've said it. I've got it off my chest. I huff and wait for Perry's response to that. There's just a click and a dial tone. He's hung up on me.

I go back upstairs and slip into my room, closing the door behind me. I set the drinks on my desk. Brian is sitting on my bed, reading something. He is so engrossed in the material that he doesn't look up when I enter the room. It takes me a minute before I realize what he's reading. In a panic, I rip the papers from his grasp. Brian is just looking up at me and he seems a little shocked.

"Tell me that's fiction," he says.

"You shouldn't have read this." My heart is pounding hard in my chest. This is bad. Real bad.

"Dawn—tell me that Perry writes fiction."

I toss the manuscript onto my desk. I am trying to think up a lie, one that would save Perry from embarrassment and at the same time not destroy my relationship with Brian. But all that goes through my mind is how screwed Perry will be if Brian goes back to school with this information and how I stand to lose Brian and my new friends.

"All these years in gym class, the changing rooms, the shower..." Brian looks away. He's thinking. "The Christmas dance..." He looks up at me with a twisted look of disgust. "I never thought I could be as freaked out as I am right now."

"Perry's a good guy." I know I should say more, but the words don't come.

"He's a fag!" Brian blurts out.

"He's my friend." I haven't been the model friend to Perry lately, but he's still my friend and I want to defend him.

"You knew about all this?"

Well yeah, I've known for about forever. I can see that Brian is just as mad at me as he is with Perry. Then just as I think he is beginning to calm down, he dodges around me and grabs the manuscript off my desk again, turning his back to me as I try to get it back. He is flipping through the pages.

"That's not yours to read!" I yell at him.

"It is when it has my name in it."

"Brian, stop!" It's not easy for a skinny little twig of a girl to compete with the broad back of a well-built athlete. "Stop it!"

I must have started shouting because the next thing I know, Mom flings the door open. We both stop and swing our heads to look at her. Her presence diffuses the moment. Resigned, Brian tosses the manuscript over to my bed and leaves. My mom steps to the side and allows him to pass, and then looks at me.

"I thought you were in trouble," she says.

"I am. But not the kind you're thinking about."

I'm looking at the manuscript now. Brian couldn't have read much, but there was enough in those few pages to condemn Perry to a living hell. If Brian speaks to Gary about this, then Perry's little secret will be all over the school by morning.

———

Now that it's morning, I try to call Perry before he gets on the bus. I'm thinking that we can skip the bus and walk to school together. Or better yet, play hooky. My stomach is twisting in knots. I'm just dreading the sound of the bus horn.

The walk down to the curb to where the bus is waiting makes me feel as though I am walking into an execution chamber. A little vomit creeps up my throat that I instantly force back down.

When I board the bus, I see Perry sitting in our usual seat, smiling at me and moving his bag to the side to make room for me. For a minute I want to sigh in relief that he isn't mad any more. But he doesn't know about the violation of his privacy yet. In less than 10 minutes, we will be stopping at Brian's house.

"I was going to ask what you thought about my manuscript, but you look as sick as a dog," Perry says. "I take it you had a busy night?"

I know that he is referring to me going all the way with Brian—which I didn't— but I really did wish he was right and that is all we have to talk about. I don't know how to break it to him about the manuscript without a hysterical outburst that will draw attention from everyone on the bus. I look over to him but say nothing. His smile fades.

"What did you do?" He practically growls at me and it's like he suspects the truth.

I look around, making sure no one is paying attention. "Brian saw it," I squeak.

For the first time in forever, I think that Perry is going to slap me. I wince in anticipation as I watch his expression turn from fury to embarrassment and back. I quietly explain how it happened and before he has a chance to respond, the bus is pulling up in front of Brian's house. I watch as Brian boards the bus, walks down the narrow aisle towards us. Before he passes us, he stops and leans down to speak to me.

"We need to talk," he says, glancing pointedly at Perry who is concentrating on the view beyond the window.

I only nod. Indeed, we do need to talk.

When we arrive at school and everyone is filing off the bus, I tell Perry to go on ahead without me and that I will catch up with him later. He goes on ahead without even acknowledging me. I walk with Brian, away from the crowds. We are far from everybody when he takes my arm. We stop and he looks me dead in the eye.

"Dawn, I really like you," he says. "But if this is going to work out between us, Perry has got to go."

I shake my head without hesitating. How dare he make me choose him over my best friend?

"You know I can't do that."

He takes a breath and makes an effort to compose himself.

"I can't pretend that I didn't read about Perry's feelings for me. I feel dirty. I can't act like nothing is wrong."

"You would never have known if you hadn't been snooping in my room last night."

"It doesn't change the facts," he spits back. "I am uncomfortable even being in the same school with him now. How do you think the rest of the guys in gym class will feel when they find out that there's a fag in the shower with them checking them out?"

In a panic I grab the sleeve of his jacket and with a voice that's both threatening and desperate I say, "You can't tell anyone about this. You will destroy him."

He jerks his arm out of my grasp. "*His* best interests are not *my* best interests. We don't need someone like that in school. What if he tries to turn other guys gay?"

All my dreams seem to shatter right here and now as I realize that Brian is an idiot. How can Perry "turn" people gay? Does he think Perry is some kind of vampire-creature? I can't believe my ears. I am furious.

"Perry was my friend before you came along and he will continue to be my friend after you've gone." My jaw is locked so tight, it starts to hurt. "If you spread this around the school, you will destroy him and he doesn't deserve that." Then without giving him a chance to respond, I turn and walk away. He doesn't try to stop me.

Later I think that maybe I shouldn't have been so aggressive; I might have been more effective in persuading Brian to keep Perry's secret. Too late to change that now.

All day, Perry avoids me while I avoid Brian and just about everyone else in Brian's crowd. It is a long day. When the time comes to board the bus, I sit alone. Perry must have chosen to walk home. The entire ride, I continue to ignore Brian and everyone else. I just want to get home.

CHAPTER 4

I wake up the next morning hoping the past events were just some horrible nightmare and that I still have my handsome boyfriend and my best friend. I follow my usual morning routine, get dressed, brush my teeth and hair and go down to breakfast. Everything seems normal.

When I get on the bus, Perry is not there. I sit alone in my usual seat as the bus continues to pick up its students. When it comes to Brian's house, he boards the bus and walks down the aisle. He hesitates and then slips in beside me. As the bus jolts forward, Brian leans in to me and speaks in a low voice.

"I'm sorry for freaking out on you and for the ultimatum," he says. "I want to be with you Dawn. If you're happy, I'm happy."

This catches me so off guard, I just stare at him like a dumb ass. When finally I speak, I have only one concern. "Did you tell anybody?"

He shakes his head. "No."

A wave of relief washes over me. Now if only I can find Perry and let him know. I'm sure he's playing hooky because he thinks his secret will be all over the school by today. I need to find him, to tell him that everything's okay.

"Where is Perry, anyway?" Brian asks, looking up and down the bus.

"I don't know."

What I do know is that I need to get off this bus and find Perry.

When the bus drops us off at school, Brian wants to come with me, but I tell him that it wouldn't be a good idea. Instead, I have him take my bag and put it in his locker for me. I make my way off the school grounds without being noticed by any of the school staff and over to the city bus stop a few blocks away. The city bus takes me across town, where I get off at a stop about ten blocks from Perry's house. I shove my hands in the pockets of my parka and walk along snow-covered pavements. At least the wind isn't blowing bitterly today.

I make it to Perry's house safely enough and knock on his door. There is no answer. I knock again, this time even harder. I see the blinds shift and wait impatiently at the door.

"Come on, Perry!" I am cold and I'm not above begging. "I know you're home!" I knock again, even harder. "Come on, I'm cold, let me in!"

The metal locks click and snap and the door is pulled open an inch. I push it wide and step inside. Perry is walking back towards the sofa, still in his pajamas. I close the door behind me and go over to the sofa to sit with him. There is a half-empty bottle of whiskey on the coffee table with a shot glass sitting next to it. I can't tell if it is left over from his mom or if Perry is drinking this early in the morning. He definitely looks like hell.

"I talked to Brian this morning," I start to say, watching him roll his eyes to the heavens. "He's not mad any more and he didn't tell anyone."

Perry just smirks. "That's the least of my concerns right now."

Now I am confused and very concerned. I've never seen him so troubled before.

"My mom is getting married again." He looks over at me. "To some asshole she met in a bar."

"I didn't know she was dating anyone."

"She's been off and on with him for almost two months."

Perry is looking around at everything except me.

"Last time I saw him, he slapped me right in front of her and she didn't say a word."

I can't believe it. Why hasn't he told me this before? I thought I knew everyone and everything in his life. Why didn't I know this? Then almost like he's reading my mind, he turns to me with a sickened look on his face.

"You didn't know because you were busy hanging out with Brian and his crowd. It's been going on since then. That's why I've been so moody."

Now I'm feeling guilty. I've been wrapped up in my own world, and I just didn't see it when my friend needed me most. That just isn't like me, and I hate myself for it.

"Do you want to stay with us?" I ask. This is a topic we've talked about before, but only as a "what if" scenario. This time I am serious.

"I don't know, Dawn." Perry seems to be too weary to think about anything at all. "We would have to talk with your mom and dad first."

"Perry, they see you as a son."

I know *my* parents won't have a problem with Perry moving in. I just don't know if his mom would actually let him go. "My mom and dad think the world of you."

"I know." Perry stares fixated at the whiskey bottle. "I need to think about this first."

"Do you want me to talk to them?"

"No." He looks back to me, his eyes bloodshot. "Not yet."

I heave a sigh and sit back, reclining into the sofa. I won't say anything to my parents until he wants me to. I don't want to give him another reason to be mad at me by opening my mouth when he's asked me not to. He reclines back into the soft cushions of the sofa too, and somehow our heads roll in together until they're touching.

"How about if I just hang out with you today?" I say as I feel his hair mingling with mine.

"Yeah. I like that idea."

We won't be going to school.

On Valentine's Day, Brian and I are having lunch together at school and at some point during our conversation, Brian tells me that Perry has been ditching gym class all week. I think that this is odd because Perry has never mentioned it when we've been together. Come to think of it, he doesn't talk to me about much either at school or on the bus. Normally he would make comments about gym class or the boys in the shower or how Brian now showers with a towel wrapped around his waist. That's always amused him, especially as the other boys tease Brian about his insecurity.

On the way home I ask Perry how gym is going and he suddenly goes quiet.

"Brian told you, didn't he?"

"He said you haven't been there all week."

I wait patiently for him to respond. He is hesitant, and maybe a bit irritated, staring out of the window, but not really seeing what is out there. After a few minutes I realize that he isn't going to answer me. "Why can't you talk to me?"

Suddenly he swings his head around. His face is flushed and his eyes flash with rage.

"Back off Dawn!" He screams for the whole bus to hear. "You haven't given a shit about me since you've been seeing Brian. You blow me off and ignore me just to be with your new friends. You have no idea what's been going on with me, so just back off."

I jump back in shock. Where has this come from? This isn't like Perry. I'm shocked and before I've thought about what I'm saying, I'm shooting right back at him.

"I'm tired of you picking on my friends. You don't want anything to do with them. I can't even talk about them around you. Are you just jealous, is that it?"

"Don't flatter yourself, it isn't jealousy." His eyes are lined with tears of frustration. "Do you think those people would have given you the time of day if you weren't involved with Brian?"

"Don't even pretend you hate Brian," I say through grinding teeth, "when we both know you're ticked off because Brian's doing me and not you."

The entire bus falls silent. Perry's face goes pale. Even through my anger, I know that I've screwed up; I shouldn't have said that. Not here, not with Brian just three seats behind us, not on a bus full of kids that we have to see everyday.

Then, out of the silence, Gary stands up

and pointing to Perry, he shouts, "I knew it! You *were* checking out his ass!"

Brian grabs Gary and pulls him back down into his seat as the whispers and giggles and comments start to rise. At the next stop, Perry grabs his bag and climbs over me to make a run for the door. I sit back trying to absorb all that is happening, hearing "gross" and "fag" comments from the other kids; some of them are supposed to be my friends—from Brian's crowd. I look back at Brian, who shoots me a dirty look before turning back to Gary. I can't hear what he is saying, but I think that Gary is teasing Brian about the time he caught Perry checking out Brian's ass.

God, what have I done?

Brian has got off the bus at his stop, and he hasn't spoken a word to me. It feels like the bus driver is taking forever to get to my house. When we do get there, I just can't seem to get off the bus fast enough and as I step down onto the pavement, my foot hits a thin sheet of ice. Next thing I know, I'm flying forward, my bag leaving my hand, and I hit the ground with a thud. From behind me I hear a roar of laughter as I push myself up off my belly, then to my knees. I wait here, embarrassed, as the bus pulls away, taking the mocking laughter with it. My hands ache from the fall and the clumsy attempt to catch myself, and the ice at my knees is beginning to melt through the fabric of my pants. I can't help feeling that I deserve it.

At home I go straight up to my room. Dad is still at work and Mom is in some room vacuuming. I just want to hide a while.

I change out of my wet pants and into some baggy sweats. In my mind I go over the fight with Perry. I just don't have the energy to do anything more than that.

Sitting on my bed, I look out of the window where the world is covered in a blanket of white glistening snow. The sky is gray and murky with the promise of more snow. This winter seems to be lasting forever. Why does time seem to drag so much when it's cold outside?

As I go to lie down on my bed, I see Perry's manuscript on my desk. I never have gotten around to reading the whole thing. And although I really don't feel like reading right now, or doing much of anything for that matter, I take it off my desk and sit down with it anyway. I have to do something to pass the time.

CHAPTER 5

I end up falling asleep before I can finish the manuscript. But I make a point of finishing it over breakfast. It is actually a good read. I bet he could get it published if he tried. I know about a lot of the things he writes about, but there is some stuff he writes about that surprises me. I realize that I don't know him as well as I thought I did.

I put the manuscript in my bag, with every intention of talking to Perry and working things out. I need to try to fix everything and attempt to get our friendship back to normal.

I stand by the window by the front door looking out for the bus. The snow is coming down in thick flakes, with almost two inches on the ground adding to the four inches that still lies from the previous fall. The bus is running late and I am secretly hoping that school will be canceled. This would be a good "snow day." Then just as I start getting my hopes up, ready to pull off my coat, the bus appears, slowly making its way to my house.

I mush through the snow on the pavement, being extra careful of the tricky patch of ice that caught me before, and make sure I have a firm grip on the handrail going up the steps. I don't want to look stupid again.

I'm not surprised when Perry isn't on the school bus. I want to think that maybe he's stayed home because of the snow. Or his mom gave him a ride to school. And although his mom has never given him a ride to school in the past, I remain hopeful. There is a first time for everything.

My mind is racing. Surely the entire school can't know what happened on the bus yesterday afternoon? There hasn't been enough time, I tell myself.

I sit alone in our usual seat. A couple of my so-called friends ask where Perry is and some make ignorant comments. I ignore them at first, but enough is enough and I tell them to shut up because they don't know what they're talking about.

When Brian gets on the bus, he walks right past me without even acknowledging me. That stings, but I have more important issues to concern me.

I make sure I'm the first off the bus so that I can get to our locker and see if Perry's been there. Digging through my bag, I am looking for the small piece of scrap paper with the locker combination written on it. I can never remember those numbers. Finally I find it and open the lock. Perry's leather bomber jacket isn't hanging there, so I guess he hasn't come in to school today. I linger at the locker for a while, taking my time, struggling out of my heavy parka and selecting books and other stuff. I'm hoping there's a chance that I might catch him before first class. But that doesn't happen.

Halfway through the day it's obvious that Perry just isn't coming to school. By lunch time, I bag up my locker and grab my parka. I just can't finish the day. I dodge the school staff and head outside and off school grounds to take the city bus that will get me within walking distance of Perry's house.

At the end of the line, I step off the city bus into the fresh snow, knowing what a fretful trek this is going to be. The once-shoveled sidewalks are now covered in snow, making the walk difficult, especially once my socks start getting wet from the melting snow falling into my shoes. I should have worn my boots. At least dry socks would have made the walk a little more bearable.

By the time I reach Perry's house, his mom is pulling out of the driveway, probably going to the cafe where she works as a waitress. I slow my pace. I don't want her to see me. As she drives off in the opposite direction, I go on up to the house.

I knock on the door, hard enough to hurt my knuckles through my gloves. I wait and watch the drawn blinds for any movement. Perry always looks out of the window to see who's knocking before he answers the door. When there is no answer, I knock again, even harder.

"Perry!" I call out to him, hopefully loud enough for him to hear me. "Come on Perry, we need to talk."

For a moment I think that maybe he isn't home, but if he isn't in school, then where else will he be on a crappy day like this? He has to be in there.

"Please let me in. I'm sorry. None of this should have happened. We need to talk."

I stand around for a good 20 minutes knocking and talking to the door. There is no answer. Maybe he went to school late and I just didn't see him. It is possible. I guess I'll just have to head back to school and find out.

I trudge back to the bus stop. My previous footprints are already filling with new snow. I make it to the corner where the bus will stop to pick me up, and clear a spot on the bench to wait. This is just a lousy day.

I make it back to school in time for the last class of the day. Walking through the school in wet socks is torture. I stop by my locker to find a book and head off to math. Brian is already sitting next to Gary at the far side of the room and as always I get stuck next to Carla. I sit down and open my book, trying to look busy so that she will leave me alone.

"Is it true?"

I look up and Carla is leaning over towards me. Her eyes are all wide and curious and she is fighting back a grin.

"Is what true?"

"That Perry's gay?"

I want to slap her around the head with my heavy math book, but instead I just sigh. "What have you heard?"

"The rumor is that Perry has a secret crush on Brian and half the football team." Carla is enjoying this. "Is it true that the only reason Perry is taking gym is to check out all the guys in the shower? I hear Perry is always the last one out of the shower."

I drop my head into my hands. This is a school with over 400 students and nasty rumors get around fast. Especially once they've been embellished to make them even more hurtful.

"Carla," I look her dead in the eye. "Are you really going to believe everything you hear?"

She pulls her head back and drops her grin, appearing somewhat disappointed.

"But everyone's talking about it." She looks more confused than usual. "What about Perry hiding in the toilet stall with a picture of Brian, doing… you know?"

"No, Carla, I don't know." What an idiot. "Just who happens to be your source of information anyway?"

"Gary told Terri and she told the cheerleaders. I just happened to be in the locker room when she was telling them."

I don't think I have ever been so disgusted with people. I have half a mind to walk out of class right now, but my socks are still wet and I would rather ride home on a warm bus rather than walk home in the cold.

During class I try to concentrate on my math, thinking it will make the hour pass faster. I so want to get out of here and away from these people. I can't concentrate much, and when the hour is finally over, I hurry to my locker, grab what I need and am one of the first to get on the bus.

When I get home, the first thing I do is change into dry socks. Comfortable once more, I use the phone in the kitchen to call Perry's house. I get his answering machine, and I leave a long message, begging him to call me. I wait by the phone until dinner, trying to hide my distress, but Mom seems to have a sixth sense. I guess moms do.

"Are you and Perry fighting?" Mom asks me as the three of us sit down for dinner after Dad gets home from work.

I shrug, poking at my spaghetti with my fork, not sure if I want to eat it or play with it. "I have everyone mad at me lately."

"Are you still seeing Brian?" Dad asks.

I'm sure he's hoping I will say that we've broken up. But to be honest, I don't know if we are still together or not. I don't know if Brian is just angry because I embarrassed him with that outburst on the bus. Am I supposed to assume that because he's ignoring me, we're breaking up? I've been too afraid to call him to find out what's going on. Maybe we all just need some time to ourselves.

"I don't know how to answer that one, Dad." It's all I can say.

For the rest of the week and all through the weekend, there is no word from Perry. He doesn't come to school, he won't answer his door. I've been to his house five times—and he won't return my two-dozen phone calls. Brian and all of my so-called new friends ignore me when they aren't making fun of Perry to my face. I am so frustrated and depressed. I don't think I have ever felt so alone.

It's Monday and I am now so miserable that I don't think I can make it through another day. I sit alone on the bus, ignored by Brian and his friends. When I get to my locker, I dig out the scrap paper with the combination number that I can never remember and open the door. Perry's leather bomber jacket is hanging on the hook. I feel my heart skip a beat. Perry is here.

I turn to look down both ends of the hallway and through the mass of kids scurrying about. I can't spot Perry. I shove my parka into the locker and grab the books I need and hurry off to my first class. Perry will be in that class.

I walk through the hall and down a set of stairs, mentally sorting out all the things that I am going to say and what order I will say them in. I think about what Perry might say and how he might respond to me. I have it all playing in my head. Everything is going to be all right.

As I walk towards my classroom, a swarm of kids comes flying down the hall. I have to throw myself up against the wall to avoid being knocked over. Strangely, they all seem to be running in the same direction, down the hall and towards the gym. I can't imagine what's going on. I don't care. I'm still thinking about seeing Perry. At least if everyone else is distracted, Perry and I will be able to have some time alone to talk before class starts. But from somewhere I can hear a noise.

Voices. Dozens of voices, chanting, cheering, jeering. Something is going on.

I start walking in the direction the voices are coming from. My pace quickens as I make out some of what is being said.

"Fight! Fight! Fight!"

I drop my bag to the floor to sprint down the hall, towards the crowd, towards the noise. I slam hard up against the wall of bodies and push my way through to the front. It's a struggle of elbows and shoving and cursing, but I get there.

I see a flurry of orange and white jackets—school football team jackets— punching, kicking, spitting, taunting. It's Perry in the middle of it all. I jump forward and grab at sleeves, screaming for them to stop. One by one, I recognize each individual. I pull at them, screaming their names, pleading with them to leave Perry alone. One by one, they fall back and disappear into the crowd.

I drop to my knees, my hands hovering over the bruised and bleeding shell of my friend. I want to touch him, to comfort him. I waver, looking over his shaking body, hearing his muffled sobs. He's lying on the cold, hard floor in the fetal position, knees constricting into his stomach, arms protecting his face. Out of fury, I look back at the dispersing crowd and scream at them.

"Get some help!"

Out of the corner of my eye, I see someone fighting their way through the crowd. At the sight of the orange and white jacket I start to panic, thinking that the football team is coming back to beat up Perry some more. I prepare myself to use my body as a shield to protect Perry from any further blows and then I recognize Brian. Breaking free from the crowd he's falling to his knees beside me.

"Perry!" Brian looks him over, a quick assessment of his injuries. "Perry, it's all right bro. Help is coming."

I just stare at Brian, completely dumbfound. Brian's attention is completely focused on Perry as he slowly eases him out of his fetal position, gently unfolding him.

From behind me I hear footsteps pounding down the hall. Voices yelling "Back to your classrooms!" Mr. Dubois. Teachers. Admin staff. All of them should have been here a lot sooner to put a stop to this. Where the hell were they?

In my frustration I turn to Brian. I grab his jacket sleeve and jerk him round to face me.

"Where were you?" On the verge of hysteria, I want to slap him and hit him like his friends just beat up Perry. "How could you let this happen?"

Next thing I know I am swinging my fists, hitting Brian anywhere and everywhere I can. I am screaming and ranting incoherently and wrestling with him as his hands struggle to catch my fists. Somehow he manages to grab my wrists from behind and holds me, my back against his body, crossing my arms over my chest.

"It's okay, I got her," he says, obviously talking to the teachers.

I am exhausted. I give up the struggle. I am feeling weak and helpless, yet still full of anger. I look over to Perry in time to see Mr. Dubois and Mr. Valentine haul his weak frame up from the floor, and practically carry him down the hall. My eyes are burning with warm, salty tears and my knees buckle.

Brian and I spend half the day in the office recounting what happened and who was involved. Perry is taken to the school nurse. The seven football players that were identified as his attackers are called into the office one by one. Their parents are called and they are sent home on suspension, pending further investigation.

I sit across from Brian and say nothing. My eyes hurt from crying. My face and nearly every muscle in my body ache from tension and exhaustion. I don't think I *can* talk if I want to. My voice is just gone.

After all the offenders have been sent home, Mr. Dubois comes over to speak with us. "I'll take it from here. Thank you both for stepping in and helping Perry. It could have been a lot worse."

"Is he going to be okay?" Brian asks.

"I'm sure he'll be fine. Perry will need some time off." He squats down in front of me. "He'll be all right, Dawn."

I just nod. I can't even look him in the eye. When he sees that I'm not going to respond, he pushes himself up.

"The day's almost over, so I'll give you kids a choice. Do you want to go to class or go home early? I wouldn't count it against you if you wanted to go home."

Brian stands up. I can't look at him and stare at the floor.

"I'll just go back to class."

Mr. Dubois nods and I feel him looking at me. "Dawn?"

"Home," is all I can say with the little vocal strength I can muster.

CHAPTER 6

Mom doesn't give me a hard time when I want to stay home from school the next day. She only sticks her head in the door once, with her morning routine of "Rise and shine, time for school!" Even her voice isn't chipper and annoying. I didn't even set the alarm last night. I guess I knew all along that I wasn't going to school today.

For the better half of the morning, I lie in bed, dozing. Each time I wake, I replay the fragments of the dreams I've had. As noon approaches, I decide to get out of bed and take a shower. A long, hot shower will improve my mood a bit, I think.

I step into the bathroom, stripping off my clothes at the door and start running the water. Once the water is hot and steamy, I step in and enjoy the hot flow, gradually relaxing the tension in my muscles. A piping hot shower almost always makes me feel better. I must have been in for longer than I thought, because my feet have started to prune. I get out and grab a large towel for my body and a small towel for my head, wrapping myself up snugly. I feel a little better. However, I'm not really thinking about anything that will upset me. My mind is blank.

I step up to the sink. The mirror is covered with steam. I put my hand against the glass, about to wipe the steam away. Then I stop myself. I don't want to see my reflection. I'm not sure why, I just don't.

I move on to dry and groom myself before getting dressed and going downstairs to the kitchen. My stomach is rumbling. I haven't eaten much in the past couple days. I open the refrigerator and look over its contents. Mom always keeps more food in the house than three people could possibly consume in a reasonable amount of time. And although my stomach is begging for me to grab something—anything—and put it in my mouth, nothing appeals to me. I grab a bottle of water and sip on it as I continue my search for food. The cabinets are full, but still nothing catches my interest. My stomach grumbles even harder. Finally, in the pantry I find a bag of pretzels and take a handful from the bag.

I sit at the kitchen table drinking my water and nibbling on my pretzels, thinking of nothing. The house is quiet with both my parents gone and there is simply nothing I want to do. I could watch television, but that might trigger a memory or a thought. Right now I am perfectly content with an empty head. Then the phone rings.

After a few rings I get up to answer it.

"Dawn, it's Mom. I won't be home in time to start dinner; I'm at the hospital with Grandma."

She sounds upset.

"What happened?"

"The doctors think she had a stroke. I called your dad and he's on his way down here to wait with me."

A sudden thought of Grandma lying in a hospital bed, and my mind comes alive with thoughts and worries. For the first time today, I am feeling something. An emotion.

"Will she be okay?"

I wonder if I should go down to the hospital. Grandma is an eighty-seven-year-old diabetic with a bad heart. What if this is it for her?

"She's stable now. Just stay home and I'll keep you posted."

Something in Mom's voice tells me that she isn't so sure. Plus, I know that she would never have called Dad out of work unless it's something very serious. Still, I know that Mom will call me if she thinks it's time to say our final good-byes.

"I'll be here."

I hang up the phone and just stand still for a moment, remembering the last time I saw Grandma. It was on her birthday last November. Come to think of it, I didn't even see her at Christmas. I was too preoccupied with Brian and Perry and skipped out on the celebration with my relatives. In hindsight, that was a lousy thing to do.

I flop onto the couch with the remote control in my hand, flipping through the channels, trying to find a show I can focus on to avoid thinking the worst about Grandma. I end up settling for reruns on a sitcom channel. Yeah, I've seen all these shows before, but they are still a welcome distraction.

At some point in the afternoon, I fall asleep on the couch. And I wake up to the sound of the doorbell. I sit up, confused. What day is it? What time is it? Where are

Mom and Dad? I rub my face, forcing myself to wake up. The doorbell sounds again. I push myself up off the couch and walk over to the front door, stopping to raise my eye to the peep hole. Standing on my porch is Brian in his orange and white school jacket and matching knit hat and gloves. His face is red from the cold and he is shivering a little.

Brian is the last person I want to see right now. Not only am I still angry with him, I am still suffering from the embarrassment of my outburst yesterday. Why is he here? Does he want to check up on me because I stayed home from school today? Does he have some sort of news from school about the incident? Sure I am curious, but I still don't want to see him. I wonder how long it will take for him to give up and go away. I stand quietly at the door as he knocks three times, hard against the wood, and calls out my name.

"Dawn!" He shouts it loud enough so that I would hear him even if I were upstairs in the shower. "Dawn, please. I need to talk to you. Please open the door."

He sounds so polite and sincere. I feel a small pang of guilt for making him wait outside in the cold. I'm sure the temperature is in the single digits out there. And here I am in my nice warm house... Okay, fine. I'll let him in and see what he has to say. The least I can do is give him five minutes of my time. Five minutes and then he's out of here.

I open the door with some attitude and step back, motioning with my hand for him to come inside. He seems surprised that I let him in—but not as surprised as I am. I close the door and stand facing him, crossing my arms over my chest, looking at him. He has with him a familiar backpack in one hand. When he steps inside, he drops it off next to the door.

"Perry left this at school. I told Mr. Dubois that I would return it to him." He looks at the bag and back to me. "When I didn't see you in school today, I was worried." He grabs the orange hat from his head and pulls off his gloves. "Are you okay?"

I sigh and turn to walk over to the couch. Without looking back, I know he is following me. I sit down on one end of the couch and he sits down on the other end. I am grateful for the space. I'm not ready to sit too close to him. I can't even look at him when I speak.

"I'm not feeling too well."

He bobs his head, thinking, listening, hesitating. I can tell there is something else on his mind. Something that I don't want to talk about. He looks over at me a few times, I catch his glances and look away.

"We need to talk about what happened yesterday."

"I don't want to talk about it."

"We have to," he says more urgently. "Dawn, I wasn't involved in what happened yesterday. By the time I found out, it was too late. I went there to stop it."

I look at him, trying to read his face. Is he telling the truth? He wasn't one of the boys beating on Perry and he did try to help Perry when he was down. I want to respond, but I feel my throat tighten and am afraid that if I speak, I will break out crying. I know that Brian isn't a bad guy; he just needs to be more selective about who he calls his friends.

"Perry didn't deserve that." I mumble.

"I know he didn't." He inches a little closer to me. "Have you spoken to him?"

I shake my head. "I've been trying to get hold of him for sometime now. He won't answer the door or return my calls."

But I haven't tried since yesterday. I should have gone to the school nurse with him, or gone by his house again or called again. I should have done something to show Perry that I still care.

The phone rings and it startles me. First thoughts are of Grandma in the hospital.

"Could that be him?"

"No."

I jump up and walk to the kitchen.

"My Grandma's in the hospital. My mom is keeping me posted on her condition."

On the third ring, I snatch the phone off the wall. "Hello, Mom?" For a moment there is nothing but silence. Maybe I let the phone ring too long and she hung up or maybe there is a bad connection. "Hello?"

"Hey, Dawn."

The male voice at the other end of the line sounds only too familiar.

"Perry?"

"I'm not disturbing you, am I?"

His voice sounds so calm and friendly. I haven't heard this voice in so long, I had almost forgotten what it sounds like.

"No, not at all. I've been worried about you."

I take the phone and look into the living room where Brian is sitting on the couch, and motion to him. He gets up and quietly walks into the kitchen and waits. I put my finger to my lips and he nods, understanding my gesture to stay quiet.

"No worries, I'm fine." Perry says. "I know you have been leaving messages and stopping by. I shouldn't have given you the cold shoulder like that. I'm sorry."

"I deserve it." I know that now is my time to pour out my heart to him. "Perry, I am so sorry about everything. I don't want to fight any more. I want things to go back to how they were with us."

"Dawn, it's okay." His tone is so calm, so forgiving. "Everything's okay."

I should feel a wave of relief, but instead I am feeling a twist in my gut. I can't quite put my finger on it, but something isn't right.

"Perry, are you okay? Can I come over?"

"Yes, I'm okay—and no, you don't need to come over."

"I know I don't *need* to—I *want* to."

"Have you read my manuscript yet?"

"Yes. I think it's great. You should get it published."

Perry chuckles. "Do me a favor? If you believe that it is really that good, can *you* find a publisher?"

"Of course!"

"But first I want to change the ending. I was hoping you could help with that."

"Sure, that would be fun."

Perry goes quiet. My stomach twists again as I wait out the silence.

"Dawn—you know I've never stopped

loving you, right?"

There's a change in his voice. And there goes my stomach again, feeling as though I can vomit right here on the spot.

"Perry," I try to compose myself. "What's going on?"

"I just wanted you to know that I love you." He pauses. "And by the way, Brian is a good guy. You should give him another chance. He really does care about you."

I look over at Brian who is leaning his back against the wall, watching me, listening, waiting.

"Perry?"

"You are the best thing that ever happened to me, Dawn. For that, I will always love you."

"Perry..." I want to say more in my weak voice, but it is too late. He hangs up. I put the phone down and turn to Brian with a sense of urgency. "Do you have the car?"

"Yeah."

"I need you to take me to Perry's house. Something's wrong."

"Let's go."

Brian gets his hat and gloves and hurries out to start the car as I put on my shoes and coat. Before heading out the door, I check my pocket for my house key and then lock the door behind me, walking steadily down the slippery pavement to the car.

Fighting the sickening knots in my stomach, I tell Brian how to get to Perry's house and the fastest way to get there. Brian drives as fast as he dares on the icy roads.

We pull up in front of Perry's house in a matter of minutes and I jump out before Brian has the chance to take the key out of the ignition. I struggle up the snow-covered walkway and up to the door. Brian is coming up behind me to stand at the door with me. I try the knob. It's locked. Just as I raise my fist to knock, there is a loud crack.

I jump. My hand is frozen in the ready to knock position. I look at Brian; his eyes are wide and I watch all the color drain from his face. Time seems to stop.

I can only stand and watch as Brian wrestles with the door, slamming it with his shoulder, kicking the solid oak to no avail. Brian steps through the deep snow over to the window, takes off his coat and wraps it around his arm, then turning his face away, he punches through the glass. The glass gives way in large shards and falls away from the frame. Brian hops up and crawls through the window and hurries around to the door to unlock it from the inside. He grabs my hand and we walk through the clutter, stopping at the hall that leads to Perry's bedroom.

"Perry?" Brian calls out. "It's Brian and Dawn."

My stomach begins twisting with unbearable pain when there is no answer.

What *was* that sound? Why doesn't Perry answer?

Slowly, we step down the hall, looking into the side rooms as we pass. All empty. When we get to Perry's door, Brian stops to look at me, squeezing my hand. Then he pushes the door. The door creaks open, revealing a messy room and something lying on the bed. Not something; someone.

Perry is lying on his bed, eyes open, staring at the ceiling. Blood is spattered on the wall behind him, all over the *Pretty In Pink* poster. One arm is dangling off the bed and within inches of his fingertips, on the floor, is something black and shiny. A handgun.

I pull my hand free of Brian's grip and step forward, my eyes fixed on the shocking scene before me. I am vaguely aware that I am panting, that my heart is pounding hard in my chest. Nausea and rising vomit leave a bitter taste in my mouth. I can make out the blank look on Perry's face. The slack jaw and the blood on his teeth. The hole in his skull and the puddle of blood, skull and brain matter soaking his bed. I feel like I'm going to faint. Like a zombie I step over to the foot of the bed, fall to my knees and then I do throw up, all over a pile of dirty clothes. When I think my stomach should be empty, I heave again and again, until I'm sure that my guts will come out through my mouth.

From behind me, Brian pulls back my hair and hands me a dry shirt from the floor. I wipe my mouth and push myself up. Turning away from the bed, Brian puts his arms around me and walks me out of the room.

"I've called for help," he says.

Brian must have made the call when I let go of his hand to go stand by the bed. I shouldn't have done that. Now that image of Perry's defiled body will be burned forever in my mind.

In the living room we sit on the couch. I hold on to Brian like he is the only solid thing in this world. He is shaking. I can feel it, even through my own shaking. All I can think of is where the hell is that ambulance?

Pretty soon I can hear the sirens. They are getting louder, coming closer. Then I hear a noise outside, and the front door flies open. A man in uniform steps in, followed by another, both carrying bags of equipment. Brian points to the hall.

"The last bedroom," is all that he can say.

I can tell it is taking every ounce of his strength to remain calm. I think that it should be easier for him; Perry was not *his* friend. *He* did not get a close look at Perry lying back there. *He* didn't see the dead eyes, the bloody teeth, the hole, the brains, the skull fragments. *He* didn't see those things, and for that I envy him. And curse myself.

We are still sitting on the couch when the police arrive soon after the paramedics. Brian does most of the talking. I can't do more than nod or shake my head. I temporarily forget how to form words. The paramedics look me over; they tell me that I'm in shock. I can understand what the paramedics tell me. Everything else seems more like just blah, blah, blah, blah, blah, like in the Charlie Brown cartoons, where only the kids can speak real words and all of the adults speak an incomprehensible language.

After the police are done talking with Brian, they let us go. We walk back to the car, where Brian opens the door for me and helps me inside, like I'm some invalid. I sit, looking at the house. I'm watching the paramedics leave and more police cars arrive. I watch the scene for as long as I can while Brian fires up the engine and pulls away slowly down the street.

Back home, Brian opens the car door for me. I'm on autopilot. I get out of the car, and stick my hand in my pocket to retrieve my house key as I walk up to the door. I put the key into the lock and, with a twist of my wrist, I turn the knob and the door opens. Autopilot.

Inside, I slip out of my parka and shoes and curl up on the couch. My parents are still away. Brian takes off his jacket, hat and gloves and squats down in front of me.

"I'm going to call my parents," he says. "Do you need anything? Something to drink? The remote?"

I shake my head.

Brian gets up and disappears into the kitchen. I hear him talking on the phone. I can't quite understand what is being said. But it's only words. Meaningless words. Afterwards we sit on the couch together; not speaking, just sitting there as the room darkens with the setting sun. At some point Brian turns on the light and the television with the volume down so low it is barely audible.

It's getting late and Brian is trying to hold back his yawns. I am exhausted and want very badly to fall asleep, but I doubt that would happen. There's still too much of today in my mind.

There is a noise at the front door. I look over just as my parents are coming into the house, shaking snow off their coats as they step inside. Mom looks over at us on the couch. She seems surprised.

"Grandma will be okay," Mom says as she removes her coat and boots.

Dad steps in behind her and shuts the door. "You kids shouldn't be up this late on a school night."

I look over to Brian with tears in my eyes. I want to tell them, but I know that if I try to speak I will babble like a fool. The way Brian looks at me before he stands up, I can see that he understands.

"Uh, I don't quite know how to say this..." His troubled eyes look to both my parents, "Perry has killed himself."

I draw my knees into my chest and bury my face in them to weep. I can't watch my parents for their reaction, it would be too painful. I just can't bear any more pain right now.

"No..." Mom starts to cry.

"What happened?" Dad demands in a trembling voice.

"He shot himself." Brain answers, but his voice is now starting to fail him. "By the time we got to his house, it was too late."

Next thing I know, Mom is on the couch holding me and we both cry. I can hear Dad talking with Brian and at some point, I don't quite know when, Brian leaves. Then, from somewhere in the darkness of the kitchen, I can hear Dad crying.

CHAPTER 7

It's the next day. I do nothing but lie in bed, drifting in and out of sleep. After thinking last night that I would never sleep again, when it finally does come, it hits me hard. I get up once or twice to go to the bathroom and even though my stomach howls with hunger, I ignore it, preferring the empty void of sleep. Every time I wake up, my body aches and the numbness in my brain leaves me feeling weak and empty. Mom came in once in the morning to tell me that she had called the school. The school allows five days grievance for approved absences; but that is the last thing I care about.

At night, Mom comes in to my room to tell me about Dad going over to Perry's house to speak with Perry's mom. Perry's mom can't afford a wake or a funeral. That is no surprise to me. She can afford all the alcohol in the world, but she can't afford to keep food in her house or pay for her own son's funeral. I start to get angry with Perry's mom, until Mom tells me that Dad is offering to pay for the funeral. Somehow that brought me some relief. Perry's mom never did much for him while he was alive, and she isn't about to start now. In fact, she is letting Dad take care of all the arrangements.

Mom's on my bed telling me all this and when she is done, she just sits there. She's waiting for me to say something, but I have nothing to say.

"We loved him too, Dawn."

Why did she say that? I know she did. They both did, Mom and Dad. Does she want to make me cry some more? No—she just wants me to know, that's all.

"We'll get through this together." Mom's voice is shaking.

I roll over; I don't want her to see the tears running down my cheeks. I just want to sleep and forget. It takes energy to cry and I just don't have that energy. But when she leaves the room, I find enough to cry myself back to sleep.

It's three days before the funeral takes place. That's three days of lying in bed, or on the couch in front of the television, in the same pajamas, just existing. I feel safe in the comfort of my own home. I don't have to see anyone or talk to anyone. At some point during those three days, I've managed to carry Perry's bag up to my room and toss it into a corner. Having it there, it makes me feel like he might be coming back for it somehow. Wishful thinking, but it brings me some odd comfort.

My parents are being kept busy between Grandma in the hospital and the funeral arrangements. They give me lots of space when they are home and only speak to try to get me to eat something. I just don't have the energy it would take to chew and swallow. I can't stand the thought of eating.

Now it's the day of the funeral, and I don't want to leave the house. I don't want to talk to people, to view Perry's body in an open casket, or see others cry. I don't want to go. I feel like I'm the worst person in the world for not wanting to go to my best friend's funeral. But I feel that by going, it makes it all real. Perry is dead. I am alone. Going will only make me face reality.

There is a knock at my door. I look up from my pillow to see Dad, all dressed up in one of his best suits. He sits down on the edge of the bed and with one hand he sweeps the hair out of my face.

"We leave in an hour," he says. "This is going to be hard, Dawn, but you need to do this. This is the last time you will get to say good-bye and if you don't go, you will regret it for the rest of your life."

The rest of my life. I just can't see that far ahead.

"Get up, take a shower and get dressed." It's more of an order than a request. "We'll be waiting downstairs for you."

Dad leaves me. He knows that I will do as he says, for Perry as much as for him and Mom. I look deep inside myself for the strength to push my weary body up off the bed. Get up. Fine, I'm up. A good shower will help me. After three days in the same clothes, I definitely need one. Okay Dad, I'll shower and dress. I'll do it, but I'm not going to like it.

I sit in the back of Dad's car on the way to Mason Funeral Home. I don't notice the ride and pretty soon we pull into the parking lot. There are quite a few cars. I doubt they are all for Perry. He didn't know a lot of people.

I walk behind Mom and Dad. Maybe no one will notice me or speak to me if I'm hiding behind them. That's what I want. It seems to work.

As we approach the room set aside for Perry, I stop at the open doors while Mom and Dad sign the guest book. From here I can see the casket on display.

One of the funeral attendants—I'm assuming a Mason, since this is a family-owned business—is standing outside the doors, greeting the mourners and asking them to sign the book. He is speaking to my parents in a soft voice, a comforting tone for mourners. It makes me feel sick. I take the pen from the book and look over the signatures. I recognize a few of them; Brian and Carla, and then the names of a few teachers. I don't see Perry's mom's signature. Maybe she isn't here yet.

I sign my name and avoid looking at the attendant with his sickening, soft, understanding smile. I wander over to stand in the open doorway and hover, counting heads, looking to see who is where. I see a lot of familiar faces. I can't help but feel that we're all dressed up like we are at a freaking party and not a funeral. At the far end of the room, a dark oak casket with gold trim is laid out surrounded by flowers. Not too many flowers. The biggest arrangement is from our school. The small arrangements scattered around the casket are those picked out by Mom. One end of the casket is open, revealing the white satin liner. And the object of my fear. My heart is pounding in my chest, I have to remind myself to breathe. Inhale. Exhale. I can't do this. I want to run. Just turn around and run away.

"Dawn?"

I jump. I turn to the familiar voice and familiar face and look at him. I know this person. What's his name? I know his name. Of course, it's Brian. A brief smile curls one corner of his mouth.

"You look like you need a hand to hold."

I look down as he holds out his hand to me. Maybe a familiar touch will bring some comfort. Maybe it will be the distraction I need. I reach out and he closes his fingers gently around my hand. I am surprised to see him here. I am surprised to see Carla and the teachers. They are mostly here out of a sense of obligation. Perry really didn't have many people to care for him. There are still many empty seats in this room, the smallest room available.

I walk with Brian around the laid-out seats and up towards the front where Carla is talking with Mr. Valentine. I try not to look over at the casket. We are so close now that I am afraid I might accidentally see what lies inside.

"I'm so sorry for your loss," Mr. Valentine says, laying a gentle hand on my shoulder. "If you need anything, I'm here for you."

How am I supposed to respond to that? "Thanks."

"Have you seen him yet?" Carla says.

"What?" I look at her.

"They did a good job with the make-up, you can't even tell..."

"Carla!" Brian interrupts.

A look of disgust is written all over my face, but I know Carla just doesn't think before she speaks. She is an idiot.

"I'm sorry," Carla says as she is ushered away by Mr. Valentine.

"She doesn't think," Brian says, shaking his head. "Do you want to see Perry before the service begins?"

Brian motions to the priest who is entering the room. I look the room over once more. I guess this is all who will be attending. This is all there is for Perry, my best friend. I glance over at the casket. I feel like Perry's spirit is calling me over to say hi. Stupid, I know, but...

I hold Brian's hand a little tighter. Maybe I can draw from him the strength I need to walk by the casket and peek inside. I know

I have to go over there. "Come with me?" I ask him.

"Sure."

Slowly, we walk up to the casket, a shiny wooden box containing my friend. I am afraid that once I look into the box, I will scream or burst out crying or faint. And I can't do that. Perry deserves better. I look into the casket and there, surrounded by white satin, his head resting on a small white satin pillow, lies my friend—the shell of my friend.

I look at his face and study the make-up. He looks more like a doll. The hair is arranged to hide the sewn up hole in his head. The suit he is wearing, furnished by my parents, is dark blue and would have complemented his eyes. I look at his hands, folded peacefully over his stomach, and for a moment I think I see a finger twitch. I stare harder, watching his chest, thinking if I stare hard enough I might see him still breathing. And I do see this; I see what I want to see. But I know it's just my mind playing tricks on me. Horrible, cruel tricks.

The person in the casket looks like Perry, but it isn't Perry. It's just an empty shell resembling Perry. I wonder if it's right to mourn a shell. I reach out my hand and touch him, slowly extending my fingers to stroke his cheek. He is cold to the touch. Do I really expect it to be any different? This isn't real. This isn't Perry.

The priest is up at the podium, waiting for the mourners to be seated, so he can begin the service and read his prepared eulogy. Brian and I take our seats in the front row, next to my mom and dad, as the service begins with a prayer. I let go of Brian's hand. I've been holding onto him so tight our palms have become sweaty.

I bow my head and pretend to go along with the prayer, and when the priest begins his eulogy I just stare at the casket. Even though I believe the priest is trying to deliver a fitting service, it was a short one. The day seems to be lacking in grand gestures for Perry. So when the time comes for the priest to invite family and friends up to give their own personal farewell or relate a special memory, even I don't volunteer.

In less than an hour, we are all going our separate ways and climbing into our cars, waiting for the hearse to lead the way to the burial site down the road. There is still no sign of Perry's mom. Whatever her reasons for not coming, it's left me feeling bitter, but at the same time somehow envious.

The drive through the cemetery is a long one. Over a thousand acres of stones, mausoleums, tributes and resting sites. There are small paved roads running throughout the cemetery, making visitation easy and accessible. There is some cleared land offering burial sites for sale to those who want to plan ahead. This is The Hills of Rest Cemetery.

Once we come to the burial site, we all park in one line and wait around the cars as the casket is set up where the pit has been dug. After about 20 minutes we are all escorted to the site where Perry will be laid to rest forever in the cold, dark ground.

Flowers have been set up around the grave and on top of the casket. It is cold and everyone is bundled up in gloves and hats and coats that cover the Sunday-best funeral clothes. I'm glad. People shouldn't dress up like they're ready to party when the occasion is a funeral.

I close my eyes and listen to the priest as he speaks. It's a speech like those I've heard in the movies. As I listen to the priest's prayers, I wonder how my parents were able to convince a Catholic priest to preside over a homosexual boy who's committed suicide. For that matter, Perry really wasn't Catholic, or even religious. I will definitely have to ask about this someday.

"...We commend to Almighty God our brother Perry Daniels; and we commit his body to the ground; earth to earth, ashes to ashes, dust to dust. The Lord bless him and keep him, the Lord make his face to shine upon him and be gracious unto him and give him peace. Amen."

In the still cold air of the day, the priest pushes his toe to a lever and the casket starts to descend slowly into the ground. Everyone stands still, silently watching. And Perry is gone.

CHAPTER 8

When we get back home, I go straight up to my room. I am too exhausted to do anything other than merely exist. Hell, I don't even want to do that. As soon as I close my bedroom door, I start taking off my black mourning clothes, dropping them onto the floor. I'm not even kicking them to the side. I lift my heavy bathrobe off the hook on my door and slip it on. Wrapping myself in the comfort of its warmth and tying the sash tightly about my waist, I drop down onto my bed and lay back, closing my eyes. Inhale, exhale. All I need to do is breathe.

Inhale.

I have to clear my mind.

Exhale.

Don't think.

Inhale.

Don't remember.

Exhale.

Just don't.

I want to fall asleep, but it seems like no matter how long I lie here, I just can't slip away. My eyes keep opening. I don't want them to open. My body just isn't ready to call it a day. For some reason, I think of Perry's bag sitting in the corner. It's been in the house for days and I have yet to rummage through it. Should I even *be* rummaging through it?

I sit up and look at the bag. There is nothing special about it; it's just a blue and gray bag full of school books. I get up and walk over to it. Kneeling down on both knees,

I touch the zipper. I shouldn't do this. What might I see?

I pull the zipper and open the bag. There's a math book, a social studies book and a few notebooks and folders. I finger through the notebooks until I find one that catches my attention. Written on the cover in black marker is: JOURNAL—GRADE 10 in large bold letters. Somehow this is morbidly enticing. I pluck it out and take it back to my bed.

I'm holding the notebook. Why did I take this damn thing? What does it matter now what Perry wrote, who knows how long ago? There can't be anything written in it that I wouldn't already know. Recollections, memories, feelings—all just words on paper of things that have already happened. I keep telling myself that it *is* just words on paper. But then, why am I so afraid of it?

I sit on my bed with the notebook on my lap. What I'm about to do would be a serious violation of privacy had Perry been alive. He had never dared to peek into my diary and

I had always shown him the same respect. But if I took it back to his house, would his mom read it? Who should read it—a person who loved him for who he was or a blood-relative who couldn't care less?

I open the notebook, turning the page to the first entry, and skim the page before reading it through. Perry always had such nice handwriting. I read through the pages; some entries are a sentence or two, others are a page long. I am familiar with most of the happenings, good and bad. I remember them. There are, as I'd suspected, few surprises. That is, until I come to read the last few entries:

December 20
Mom's going on a vacation this week-end with Mike. I don't know what she sees in him. Sure, he makes good money but he treats her like crap. The only time they seem to get along is when they are both drunk. Hopefully he's just another one of her flings and won't last very long. The Christmas dance is tonight. I can't wait. I have

the perfect hairstyle for Dawn. Her dress is so beautiful! I can't wait to see what Brian will be wearing tonight. I wonder if I can pretend that Brian is my date without him knowing?

December 23
Okay, so the Christmas dance was a disaster. For me anyway. First, I never thought I would feel the jealousy I felt with Dawn and Brian. Something just ate at me. Then Gary caught me looking at Brian's rear! I have never been so careless, but Brian was bent over and well, I just couldn't help myself. I get so tired of hiding who I am. I just feel like I need some kind of release before I explode.

Then when I got home, Mike was there and he started getting at me about coming home so late. I don't know who he thinks he is. He's not my dad. For some reason, I snitched a bottle of whiskey from the cupboard and walked over to Dawn's house, slugging the bottle dry. Yeah, it was stupid of me. But at least I don't get ridiculed over there when I mess up.

December 26
I tried talking to Mom about getting help for her drinking problem. Maybe I should have done this while she was sober. She started going on again about how it was Dad's fault for ruining her life. She must have called him every foul word she could think of. I couldn't take it. I called Dawn, but she wasn't home. She was probably out with Brian again. I know I should be happy for her, but I can't help feeling that Brian is taking away my only friend. I just don't know what I would do without Dawn.

December 28
That bastard! I can't believe he freaking hit me! And Mom didn't say a word. Who does he think he is? Where the hell is Dawn?

December 30
Brian, Brian, Brian! I am so freaking

tired of hearing about Brian! I really needed you tonight Dawn and you were too busy messing around with Brian. My back hurts. I think Mike left bruises this time. I thought Mom kept a stock of painkillers for her hangovers, but I can't find anything. I'll just have to see what I can scavenge from the cupboard.

January 3

Ditched again. Dawn wouldn't even talk on the phone with me because Brian was there. What does she see in him? What did I see in him?

January 15

Dawn came over today. Mom and Mike were off somewhere for the weekend. I was happy to see her, but it seemed as if Dawn didn't really want to be here. I was hoping to talk to her about what's been going on— but we don't seem to communicate like we used to. I was hoping that she would ask me what was wrong with me. But she just didn't notice or care.

Maybe I should've said something. I mean, she wouldn't come over if she didn't still care for me, right?

January 18
I don't know how much more of this I can take. Mom is marrying that asshole and I'm losing my only friend to those jerks at school. For God's sake! How much more of this can I take?

February 11
I think Mike cracked a rib. God this hurts! I want to go to the hospital, but I'm afraid to. If I go they will see the other bruises. I'll have to ditch gym for a while. I'll see if I can steal a bottle of painkillers from the school nurse tomorrow. Until then, I'll just try to numb the pain with what I can.

February 17
I can't believe Dawn outed me in front of everyone on the school bus! The nerve of her! How can I even show my face in school again?

February 18

I think I'm turning into my mom. I've been drinking more than she has lately. She gets so wasted, she doesn't remember how much she goes through. Today she asked me about some missing bottles and I said the booze has been going down faster since Mike moved in. She believed me! She would be so ticked if she found out it's been me drinking her whiskey. Mom and Mike have been married for a week now and he has already given her a black eye. Serves her right. I have a little buzz going right now, so I'm not feeling much of anything.

February 19

Got my ass beat in school by a bunch of jocks. Thank you Dawn for making my life even harder. First it was the laughing and insults and now this. I haven't talked to Dawn in days and I don't care to either. The other day, Mom and Mike got into a fight and Mike put a gun to Mom's head. When I tried to intervene, he turned the gun on me, pressing the barrel right into my temple. You know what? I wasn't scared. I didn't care. I just thought finally I would have some peace. I think a part of me wanted him to pull the trigger. I found out where Mike keeps his gun. I had it out today, playing with it. Maybe I should have it waiting for him when he comes home.

February 21
I know what I have to do. For the first time in a very long time, I feel peaceful. My mind has never been so clear.

I've read it. I'm sitting here. I stop breathing—I don't know for how long. My eyes start to dry before I realize I'm not even blinking. It's like my whole body has just ceased to function. Breathe in... out... blink, breathe in... out... blink...

Why didn't I see this coming? All the signs were there. Why couldn't I have done something?

Perry was just so angry with me. I did try to talk to him, didn't I? Think, Dawn, think! Maybe if I'd tried harder, put more effort into finding him, pounded on his door harder, called his house more, busted out his bedroom window to crawl inside and force him to talk with me... There were so many things I could've done. Should have done. Why didn't I do them? Why didn't I tell Perry that I loved him back?

Maybe if I'd never got involved with Brian or never brought home Perry's personal life story and laid it on my desk out in the open for Brian to see. Brian. What a dirty word his name's become to me now. I can't say it any more without it leaving a foul taste in my mouth. Everything is because of Brian. If only it had stayed just the two of us, Perry and me, none of this would have happened. We were happy. We could have stayed happy. Damn you Brian!

I grab the notebook and fling it across the room. It flaps through the air and slides across my desk and onto the floor along with some other papers that were on my desk. That isn't enough though.

In a rage I grab handfuls of my quilt and pull it off the bed. Then my pillows, throwing them across the room. My bed sheets, the clock radio, the lamp and everything else I can get my hands on—are all thrown across the room. I tear the posters down from my walls and shred them, crushing them in my fists and throwing them to the floor. I pull out dresser drawers and fling them, with all my strength, against the wall, cracking the wood and the plaster.

Still, it isn't enough.

I grab all my perfume bottles, ceramic and glass knick knacks and shatter them against the wall. Almost. Then as I grab the chair from under my desk and lift it as high as I can to take out my frustrations on the dresser mirror, the door swings open and my mom and dad stand in the doorway with their faces frozen in fear and shock. I stop. Suddenly I feel weak, and I drop the chair.

Mom walks in with her arms reaching out to me. Her eyes are red from crying all day and her face is worn and tired. She has never looked as old as she does right now. I just stand there, knowing that as soon as those loving hands touch me, I will break. And then I fall into Mom's embrace and I cry. I cry until it hurts. I cry harder when I feel Dad come up behind me and wrap his arms around me and Mom. Yet, even in the loving arms of my mom and dad, I feel alone.

Shortly after the funeral, Mom booked my first session with a therapist.

Therapy is a load of crap if you ask me. Dr. Reed reminds me of a fake talk show host who thinks he has all the answers to everyone's problems. I'm not even going to try to remember his name. He sits across from me with that serious look on his face, his bald head catching the glare of the fluorescent lights.

With his notebook in his lap and a pen in his hand, he asks me the dumbest questions. How did I feel when Perry and I fought? How did I feel when he died? What did I feel when I saw his body on the bed? Am I having suicidal thoughts?

All I can think of is that this man is an ass. Mom is paying him good money and what for? For me to learn how upset I am about losing my best friend? To learn how it was my fault that Perry took his life? She needs to pay money for me to discover this?

I had four sessions with Dr. Reed before I went back to school. Four wasted hours that would have been better spent staying home in bed or on the couch, brooding. Nevertheless, he has convinced Mom that we are making progress and that I should return to see him twice a week.

CHAPTER 9

So, here I am, hiding in a toilet stall at school. I'm sitting here, and my legs are numb from sitting. I've been here for what, hours? I'm not even sure what time it is and I don't really care. I just know that I need to get up and get some circulation back into my legs. All I can do is stand for a few minutes, my legs are feeling so dead. Then the pins and needles come, thousands of them pricking my legs from thigh to toe. And although I cringe in agony at the sensation, I realize this is the first time in weeks that I've felt anything at all.

Slowly, I make my way out of the stall, and walk to the sinks and back. I'm walking in circles just to keep my legs moving, to get rid of this discomfort.

I avoid the mirrors as I take this repetitive path from the sink to the stall. Back and forth, back and forth. I wonder, briefly, what it would be like to see myself in the mirror. It's been a long time. How would I look? How would I feel? But I'm still not ready to face myself.

Once the pain is gone, I go to collect my books and step out into the hall. The hall is empty; the school is quiet and half the lights are off. It's all rather eerie.

I walk over to the nearest classroom to peer in at the clock. Quarter to five. I've missed the bus and most of the students and teachers involved in extracurricular activities will be on their way home by now. Looks like I'll be walking.

I make it down to my locker undisturbed. I drop my books into the bottom and reach out for my parka, but my eyes are drawn to the brown bomber jacket hanging opposite.

I lift the leather jacket off the hook and slip it on. Although it fits loosely on my slender frame, it is warm and comfortable. The scent of Perry's cologne still lingers. I close my eyes and take a deep whiff. I smile. God I miss you Perry.

Standing there in the hall, I realize that I don't want to go home. But where do I go? I shove my hands in the jacket pockets and begin walking down the hall. I come across the staircase that leads down to the gym. No one will be there now. I walk along the hall, past the locker rooms. Half the lights are on. The school never turns off all the lights. At the end of the hall I come to the pool entrance. I walk along the edge of the pool, peering down into the still, blue water. It looks cool and peaceful.

Inviting.

Almost hypnotizing.

Quiet.

This is nice. This is what I want. This is what I need. With one hand I grab the collar of Perry's coat and raise it to my nose, just enough to take in a big scented breath. Perry.

I smile.

Without hesitating, I step forward, plunging into the cold, blue water with a loud splash. I relax, letting the water soak my clothes, adding weight, dragging me deeper below the surface. My eyes are open as I sink to the bottom. And with the cold, hard bottom of the pool against my back, I think of Perry. His scent. His laugh. I am holding my breath, but I really want to let go.

I let go.

I open my mouth and breathe in the water and all its chemicals. My body jerks from the force of the water filling my lungs. I can't breathe. My body wants to stay alive. Survival is a natural instinct. I'm fighting against it. I start to black out. This is it.

I hear a noise. A splash. Something is coming down towards me. A figure.

Perry?

I open my eyes. There's a light, a face. I'm wet, lying on a hard floor. Am I still in the water? I cough, expelling liquid from my lungs, and try to focus on the face floating above mine. There are voices. Then darkness.

"Can you hear me?" A voice is calling to me through the blackness. "Dawn! Open your eyes!"

I hear the voice, but I can't respond. Is it Perry? Am I dead?

"Dawn, open your eyes."

I open my eyes. There are people around me. I am strapped to a stretcher inside an ambulance. I have to focus. I look up into the soft, blue eyes of... Brian? He is leaning over me, dripping wet. I'm struggling to understand what is going on.

What's happened?

Where am I?

My mind is all muddled. It is hard to think.

"There you are." Brian smiles. "I thought I'd lost you."

I find some scrubs in a cupboard inside the hospital room and change out of my gown. Perry's coat is on a hanger. It is still wet, but that doesn't matter; I slip it on. There are a few bus tokens inside the hidden inner breast pocket. I can get into so much trouble for this, I know. No one seems to notice me as I walk pass the nurses' station. Brian is in the waiting room, speaking to the police.

I walk out of the hospital, unchallenged, into the cold and down the stone steps. It's a short walk to the corner, to the bus stop. All the time I'm feeling… something—I don't know what. I know I shouldn't have left the hospital. I should have waited for my mom and dad.

At the bus stop, I brush some snow off the bench to make a clean spot. It is cold and getting colder as the night starts to come down. There is a light, crisp wind, and it lashes bitterly through Perry's wet coat. I wait in the cold, thinking any minute now someone will come to take me back to the hospital. Any minute now. Where is that damn bus?

Then the bus arrives on time, opening its doors onto a semi-heated interior and the few passengers it is transporting. I walk to the back of the bus and settle into a seat away from the other passengers. I have a specific destination in mind and I want to be alone.

I get off the stop nearest to Perry's house. The cold through the wet leather jacket is crippling, making me feel sick.

I trudge along icy pavements and approach Perry's house, sitting back from a snow-covered yard. I imagine the path the paramedics had taken to get there. I imagine them pulling up in front of the house, followed by police cars. I imagine them rushing up the path and in through the front door. I see Brian and me sitting on the couch in the front room. And Perry lying dead on his bed.

I stop in front of Perry's house and stare at the red door.

Perry is gone and I'll have no reason to come to this house again. All of the time I've spent in this house over the years, coming to know it inside and out; all the summers, the winters, the days and the nights. All of that is just a memory now. Those times have become my past, however much they will help to shape the person I'll become. And I realize that I will have to move on.

I walk on past the house, and it feels like a weight is lifting from me. I force myself to look forward and fight the urge to look back, fight the urge to relive that horrible day. I won't look back. I have to keep walking.

It is dark by the time I get home. I walk through the door and Mom comes rushing over. It's obvious she's been out of her mind with worry.

"Are you okay?" Mom asks, kneading her hands together. "Dad's been out driving around, looking for you."

I stand there taking off the wet coat and look at her and for the first time in weeks, I speak one short sentence to her. "I'm okay, Mom."

Mom just hugs me for a while. And then, just like she has every day for the last couple of weeks, Mom tells me that she has a plate for me in the oven. Tonight, I think I'm going to try to eat something. It will be another step forward.

In the kitchen I pull the still warm plate of meat and mashed potatoes from the oven and set it on the table. I grab a fizzy drink from the refrigerator and set it down in front of my plate. I'm still not hungry and I know this food will lie heavy in my stomach, but I have to try. I never thought a person could forget how to eat, but I have to concentrate on every aspect of getting the food into my mouth and chewing and swallowing.

As I begin to pick at my mashed potatoes, I hear the front door open and close.

"She's here," I hear Mom say from the other room. "She's in the kitchen… eating."

I watch the kitchen door, waiting for one of them to appear but they don't. They give me my space and allow me to go at my own pace.

My plate is barely half-empty by the time I call it quits. My stomach is feeling a burden it hasn't felt in weeks and my jaw muscles are tired of working. I put my plate into the sink and go upstairs to change into some pajamas.

I am about to get into my bed when I

remember Perry's manuscript, still in my locker at school. Perry had asked me to do something for him.

I search around underneath my bed and pull out my notebook computer. I haven't used it for months. I hope that I can remember how. I find all the chords and plug everything in and switch on the power.

I go online and check my mail. Nothing but spam. I put my cursor in the search bar and look for publishing houses. Finding a few, I go to their home pages, looking for their information and submission guidelines. I find a few and bookmark them. Then I begin to compose an email to the first company on the list:

Dear Ms. Bourne,

I would like to send you a story about the life and death of special friend of mine...

CHAPTER 10

Two years later...

When the delivery man comes I am up in my room applying the finishing touches to my makeup. Maybe I'm wearing too much, but I have to look good for the cameras. I run downstairs, a little too quickly in heels, and almost lose my footing on the last few steps, but I catch myself just in time. My mom and dad are in the kitchen standing at the table where there is a large brown box. I think that they are more excited than I am.

Mom hands me a knife to slice through the tape. I just can't seem to open the box fast enough. I pull open the flaps and reach inside, pulling out a hardcover book. The dust jacket is colorful and has a high school picture of Perry on the front. The title of the book is *Rainbow in the Shade*.

Mom and Dad reach in to grab a copy each as my fingers examine the book in my hands, feeling the hard cover and paper pages, reassuring myself that it is real. I leaf through the pages, picking out a word here and there, and then turn the book over to read the back of the jacket. Along with a couple of quotes from book reviewers, there is a pledge to donate all proceeds from the sale of this book to troubled teens and to help families cope with suicide.

"This is wonderful!" Mom exclaims.

"Perry would be so proud," Dad says.

I smile. I don't have to say anything; I know that he would.

Mom glances at the clock and puts the book back in the box. "We'll have to admire these later if you want to graduate today."

I take the book with me as I grab my hat and gown from the couch and hurry out to the car. I read through the first and last chapters in the book, the only two chapters that I wrote, as Dad drives and Mom is fussing with the video camera. When we get to school, I leave the book in the car and run inside to meet up with my class as Mom and Dad hurry to find seats in the crowd of proud parents.

I walk past all the kids who will graduate today. I stop to speak with Carla, who is now just beautiful. Her acne has cleared up, she has cut and styled her hair—and she must have got rid of the cat because she no longer smells like cat pee. She has her arms around Gary. It's amazing to think that they've been dating for almost five months now.

I find Brian off to the side, struggling with the zipper of his gown. He sees me and he blushes. I smack his hands away from the zipper and pick out a few loose threads and zip it up for him. He's so helpless sometimes.

"Thank you," he says. "You look beautiful."

I put my arms around his neck and kiss him.

"The books came today," I tell him.

"Did you save one for me?"

"You have to come over and get it." I am feeling a bit playful.

"Oh, I'll come over. I'll sneak into your bedroom and..."

He never gets to finish because the teachers are calling to us to line up alphabetically. It is time for the graduating class to line up and prepare to file out of the door.

The last day of school. Once we are all assembled and waiting at the door for our cue, I look up and down the line. Some of these kids I've known since infants. Some of them have become good friends. Some have gone their own ways. A sudden sadness washes over me as I realize that this may be the last time I see many of them. Then it's gone, as quickly as it came.

Outside, I hear a song start playing over the speakers—*Pomp and Circumstance*. It is our cue to start moving out of the door in single file. I walk out with my classmates into the bright sun on this warm day. The only thing missing, the one thing that would make this day perfect is Perry. A lump comes to my throat momentarily. Then I think of Perry's book. Perry will always be with us through his words. I feel strangely comforted by that thought.

After today, I feel that the whole world will be opened up for me, and I'm looking forward to the future. Who knows what it might bring? I look along the line of my classmates again. I know that I belong here, with them. And I think—I feel—that Perry would be proud of me.

Life at the **CUTTING EDGE**
For more gritty reads in the same series

Breaking Dawn
DONNA SHELTON
Is friendship forever? Secrets, betrayal, remorse and suicide

The Finer Points of Becoming Machine
EMILY ANDREWS
Emily is a mess, like her suicide attempt

Marty's Diary
FRANCES CROSS
How to handle step-parents

The Only Brother
CAIAS WARD
Sibling rivalry doesn't end at the grave

Seeing Red
PETER LANCETT
The pain and the pleasure of self-harm

SADDLEBACK™
EDUCATIONAL PUBLISHING